I0628940

The Enchanted Forest

James Faber

Salem-Danvers Village Press

James Faber

Salem-Danvers Village Press

Published by Salem-Danvers Village Press, a division of Organ Group Corporation, and imprinted by New Verse, an imprint of Salem-Danvers Village Press.

NEW VERSE

First Salem-Danvers Village Press publishing/printing, December 2017.

First Edition; Paperback

Copyright © 2017
The Enchanted Forest

ISBN: 0-9984311-3-3
ISBN-13: 978-0-9984311-3-0

The Enchanted Forest

James Faber

ACKNOWLEDGMENTS

Sometimes, people do crazy things. And then there are the reasons to distrust the villains. The only people who are to be acknowledged here are the people who heard them and told them to people they knew. No one can expect anything to happen. But, as you read this, you should remember, no one can ever escape the Enchanted Forest.

The Enchanted Forest
James Faber

The Enchanted Forest

James Faber

Nothing Belongs Here

Contents

Characters
In Order of Appearance

Narrator.
The Narrator of the entire story. He could be a man. She could be a woman. It could be two people taking turns narrating. It could be William Ash and or it could be another character as well, such as Ella Lohrina.

Dorado.
A witch doctor who causes trouble.

Chorus.
People who sing.

The people who lead the village of El Dorado:
- *Village Elder 1.*
- *Village Elder 2.*
- *Village Elder 3.*
- *Village Elder 4.*

Teenagers who get into trouble:
- *Teenager 1.*
- *Teenager 2.*
- *Teenager 3.*
- *Teenager 4.*
- *Teenager 5.*

Magistrate of the Court.
The person who oversees the trial of Dorado

Lumberjacks who cut down trees:
- *Lumberjack 1.*
- *Lumberjack 2.*
- *Lumberjack 3.*
- *Lumberjack 4.*
- *Lumberjack 5.*

Danielle.
Daughter of John and member of first family who bought the house on plantation.

Larry.
The boyfriend of Danielle.

Catherine.
Daughter of John and member of first family who bought the house on plantation.

Robert.
Son of John and member of first family who bought the house on plantation.

John
Father to Danielle, Catherine, and Robert and husband to Christine.

Christine.
Mother to Danielle, Catherine, and Robert and wife to John.

Concerned Citizen.
Someone who reports a fire.

Police Dispatcher.
The police officer who answers emergency calls.

Police Deputy.
A police deputy who goes to the plantation.

Cynthia.
Daughter to Lindsay and Peter and sister to Abigail, and member of the second family of the plantation and the house.

Abigail.
Daughter to Lindsay and Peter and sister to Cynthia, and member of the second family who bought the plantation and the house.

Peter
Father of Cynthia and Abigail and husband to Lindsay, and member of the second family who bought the plantation and the house.

Lindsay.
Mother of Cynthia and Abigail and wife to Peter, and member of the second family who bought the plantation and the house.

Doctor.
The doctor at the hospital who wants to know more about the mysterious and strange death of Lindsay's husband.

Nurse.
The nurse at the hospital who wants to know more about the mysterious and strange death of Lindsay's husband.

Store Clerk.
A clerk who works at a store with boutique items and other stuff.

Hank.
The mysterious boyfriend of Abigail.

Ella Lohrina.
A fair maiden who wishes to experience more adventure.

Caterina Siterina.
The younger stepsister of Ella Lohrina.

Helenia Siterina.
The older stepsister of Ella Lohrina.

Frances Siterina.
The stepmother of Ella Lohrina.

Emily.
Someone with a red cape who goes to visit her grandmother's house.

Witch.
The person who tries to attack and kill Emily and her grandma.

Simonia Bernfurt.
The real name of the witch who tries to attack and kill Emily and her grandma.

Grandma.
Emily's grandmother

Jack's Mother.
The mother of Jack who scolds him for not listening.

Jack.
A boy who refuses to listen to his mother.

Mysterious Man.
The person who sells magic beans to Jack.

Town Crier.
The person who announces that there will be royal balls for five nights.

Charles Lohrina.
The father of Ella Lohrina and a spymaster.

John Lohrstadt.
A fellow spy and a friend of Charles Lohrina.

Herald.
The member of the royal court responsible for announcements and formal duties.

Henry David Michael.
A prince who is interested in Ella Lohrina.

Anna Rampione.
A fair maiden who is engaged to Andre Eric Michael.

Andre Eric Michael.
A prince who is engaged to Anna Rampione.

Other Narrator.
The narrator, but in a disguised voice.

ACT I

SCENE 1. El Dorado, North America. 1354
Town Square

Enter Narrator

Narrator.
People are near and they see nothing but trouble. It is a sign of people dying or someone who is participating in a despicable act of hideousness.

Enter Dorado

Dorado.
No one will find out anything. Every member of my tribe is a complete idiot because they don't know who I am actually. They can all die in hell.

Narrator.
Dorado goes further into the woods and gathers some of his ingredients so he can produce a wicked curse on people who wouldn't suspect a thing.

Enter Chorus

Chorus.
(*singing*)
It is the early spring in the fourteenth century, fourteenth century, fourteenth century, fourteenth century, century. No one suspects a thing. Dorado is up to no good and soon his own people will turn on him. He is a trouble maker. He should be burned at the stake. He is a witch and he needs to burn in hell.

Because this is the fourteenth century, were witchcraft is against the law. He shall be burned at the stake and be tied up in order to turn into ash. He is the reason why evil exists in the fourteenth century. He must die in the fourteenth century or else he will curse his land.

Dorado.
Who are you? What do you want? Speak up or show yourself. I can do whatever I want. I listen to no one. You must be some group of people who are hiding. I will hunt you down before you make things worse. You will not have me killed because I will kill everyone before I die. And then I will curse them and all people who lives on my land.

Narrator.
There is an epidemic on the loose in El Dorado. No one knows what it is or where it came from. There are some suspicions that it is from the Gods because of what is happening to the tribe led by Dorado. It is just something mysterious that just keeps on happening. Something needs to be done in order to stop this madness but no one knows how to stop it. There is no solution to anything.

Enter Village Elder 1

Village Elder 1.
Something mysterious is happening and I will find out soon. There is something just plain wrong with this picture but there is nothing but madness.

Chorus.
(*singing*)
Damnation, Holy Damnation. There is something

afoot. He will find out but he won't survive. There is a case that can't be understood. There will be smoke, there will be fire. No one will be spared. It is something that must be done. He shall be burned at the stake. He shall be no more. He shall be the end of his kind, and he shall kill every one of his kind. No one will be left. This is a Holy Damnation. Fire and brimstone will appear and it won't disappear until his ashes has been blown away by the wind.

Narrator.
Something is going to happen soon to Dorado, but he does not know it yet. It is only a matter of time until the members of his tribe figure out what is going on. It will be the end of time and he will do something awful to the rest of humanity. No one will know why something strange is happening to them, but some might recall about the legend of Dorado.

Enter Village Elder 2

Village Elder 2.
I will set out to find what is going on. I will not rest until I get to the bottom of this. There seems to be something strange and mysterious going on. It must be for some hidden agenda and we might have a traitor in our midst.

Enter Village Elder 3

Village Elder 3.
There is nothing strange going on. It is only your imagination. You are just seeing things that are not really there. It is just a waste of time to explore what you want to find out. You won't find out anything

because nothing exists. It is just your stupid mind and brain playing tricks on you. This expedition of yours will just look foolish in the end.

Enter Village Elder 4

Village Elder 4.
Here he goes again. Grandpa, the oldest of us village elders, is trying to say we are crazy again. He thinks we will all look like fools and idiots in the end because he says there is nothing there, but we will never give up.

Chorus.
(*singing*)
There is trouble afoot. No one knows what will happen. The Village Elders are fighting over something that should not be an issue. It is something that will never end. Grandpa is in trouble. He will do anything to protect whatever is happening to the tribe and will never admit defeat. But he is in trouble and will be held hostage, or something that will need to be solved in the end. It is just a witch hunt because there is nothing that can be done to convinced those other village elders. It is just a waste of time.

Narrator.
It looks like there is another problem, but people will always create something new in order to control the narrative. It is just an excuse to find out what is happening. No one will know who is doing what but that is the case to control the precise notion of an idiotic ideology.

Dorado.
No one suspects a thing. They have all turned on Grandpa. That feels like a relief but it isn't because there is something needed in order to distract everyone.

Narrator.
The Village Elders decide to retire for the rest of the day because it is almost nightfall. But, there is something that will be happening soon. It is for that reason why they won't find out until they look right in front of them. They are clueless but soon everyone will know everything. Meanwhile, there is still something that must be done. It will be something that will be a surprise to the Village Elders but probably not Grandpa. There is still something at hand. Nothing will ever be the same but it is the sane and still that must be silenced. For the time being, it is still part of nothing but craziness.

Chorus.
(*singing*)
He will survive. He will survive. Because he will never survive. He is a witch, a witch, a witch. Oh No, what's that? He is flying on a broom. He has a black pointy hat he is wearing. Is he a shaman or is he a witch. He can be both. Uh Oh, he is a witch doctor. He wants to destroy everything in sight. He wants to get rid of all the Village Elders. He wants to be in control. It is just something that he needs to do because he trusts nobody, and he wants to control everything with no one interfering with his authority. He is a witch, a witch, a witch doctor? That is a surprise. He will not anyone know, because he is a witch, a witch, a witch doctor.

Narrator.

Dorado escapes into the woods of the Enchanted
Forest of El Dorado. He continues his practicing of
witchcraft so he can maintain his power.

[Exeunt All]

SCENE 2. El Dorado, North America. 1354
Enchanted Forest

Enter Dorado

Dorado.

Eyes of frog, hair of a bat, bile of a hog, skin of a cow,
venom of a snake. Mix them all together. I will
become the one true power and I will defeat everyone.
It is something that is not the type of craziness you
have ever seen. I will reign over the death of everyone
and no one can stop me. It is I who is in charge of this
party. I rule and no one will ever stop me. I will never
give up. I will continue to engage in witchcraft until I
die or they kill me. I will not die alone. I will take
everyone done with me. It is something that needs to
stay in the place of the craziness of society.

Enter Narrator

Narrator.

Dorado is up to no good and he will not stop until he
dies or someone kills him. He is such a bad, bad
person. No one knows it yet, but he will die but no
one will know if he will die or if he is to be killed. It is
just a sign of society doing bad things in the craziness

of the things of the people in the near of the future. It is such a reality of what not to do but no one shall ever listen, and that will be the end of a moral society. He too shall overcome and stop this for the good of the people, but only in an alternate reality.

Enter Chorus

Chorus.
(*singing*)
He's up to no good. He wants to destroy the world. He shall succeed. No one will ever stop him. But wait, what's this? Uh Oh, there is something moving in the opposite direction. It must be someone who is spying. Someone needs to hide before everyone finds out. There is something that must be in the crazy society of witches. But wait, he is a witch, a witch, a witch what? He is a witch doctor. Oh No! Someone must do something and it must be now. We will not die because we shall prevail.

Narrator.
A group of teenagers go running into the woods of the Enchanted Forest because they wanted to. They were just crazy and mischievous. Call them crazy hooligans, but they were just up to no good. Nothing can stop them because they just want to act crazy. If something happens to them then something happens, and that will be the end of that.

Enter Teenager 1 and Teenager 2

Teenager 1.
I am so drunk right now.

Teenager 2.
We are going to get so lost in here that we won't ever find a way out.

Enter Teenager 3 and Teenager 4

Teenager 3.
Dream on man, we will always find a way out.

Teenager 4.
Yeah, says the person who always gets called out for doing stupid and idiotic antics.

Enter Teenager 5

Teenager 5.
So, what about me, am I one of the dudes, or do you find that crazy because I am a girl?

Teenager 3.
Stop acting like an idiot.

Teenager 5.
Says the person who always acts like an idiot.

Teenager 1.
Oh says the girl who acts like a crazy drunk.

Teenager 2.
Wait, what's that? I hear someone talking or laughing in an evil manner.

Teenager 3.
I don't hear anything.

Teenager 1.
Me either.

Teenager 4.
Someone must be delusional again.

Teenager 5.
This will be the death of us and it will haunt our families for the rest of our lives.

Narrator.
The teenagers are hiding behind the woods and they are watching Dorado engaging in witchcraft. They don't know what to think but most of them are idiots and some of them are even drunk and high on poisonous mushrooms. It is just quite something special. One of the teenagers sees something moving but decides to follow it anyway. But that will just be a mistake.

Teenager 1.
I see something moving in the bushes.

Teenager 2.
Don't get yourself killed.

Narrator.
One of the teenagers goes into Dorado's hiding place and he is baffled of what he is able to see. All of the other teenagers runs towards him to see what is happening.

Teenager 1.
Run, as first as you can.

Teenager 3.
Run, from what?

Teenager 1.
Whatever is behind you. There is someone behind you, so don't move.

Teenager 5.
I see nothing. You must be seeing stuff again.

Teenager 4.
Don't look behind you.

Dorado.
I see I have company. That is good. Now I can hold you hostage.

Teenager 5.
Who said that?

Dorado.
Me. Look behind you.

Teenager 5.
I'm getting out of here.

Dorado.
You can run but I will always find you.

Narrator.
There was a loud thump that came from deep within the woods of the Enchanted Forest, which was followed by loud screams, all in the name of something sinister. Dead silence followed afterwards.

No one was ever heard again.

Teenager 5.
What are you doing to us, and why you tied us all up
to trees and wooden stakes.

Dorado.
My dear child, you and your friends are going to die
tonight. You will be a sacrifice to the devil himself.
No one can escape me, and I will kill you all.

Narrator.
Dorado performs a satanic ritual so he can practice his
powers of witchcraft.

Chorus.
(*singing*)
There has been a sacrifice, a sacrifice, a satanic
sacrifice. No one will suspect a thing. People won't
care. Dorado has killed five people and he won't stop
until he is dead. But that is not the end of Dorado. He
will face his justice soon and he shall be executed so
that no one will ever be killed in an evil manner again.
But, he shall have his revenge. He shall impose all
types of sacrifices upon his death. Before he dies he
shall curse every person who opposes him. He will get
his way and he shall make sure he has his justice.
Good riddance, but that is not the end of Dorado.

Narrator.
The torches burn out instantly. It is now completely
dark. And then something can be heard. The torches
are then instantly lit again by magic. Everything is
going as planned for Dorado, as he will never give up.
He is a bad guy that you should not mess with. But he

will never learn. Then suddenly, the torches go out again. Winds are now blowing at high speeds, clouds are forming to a darker color, and lightning and thunder starts to appear. The torches go out again, and this time screams can be heard. And then, the torches are lit by magic again. All that is left is the skeletons of the five teenagers, which then turn to ash as Dorado touches each of them.

[Exeunt All]

SCENE 3. El Dorado, North America. 1354 ## Enchanted Forest. Five Months Later.

Enter Narrator and Village Elder 1

Narrator.
Five months has passed since the killing of those five teenagers by Dorado. Something is going on. The Village Elders have noticed that Dorado has kept disappearing after failing to appear at several tribal meetings. It is for that reason why some of the elders decide to find Dorado.

Village Elder 1.
I am going to find out were Dorado is before the rest of our people find out.

Narrator.
The first Village Elder begins his journey and he can hear what sounds like Dorado singing and chanting. But he wants to know if it is really Dorado. And then, suddenly, something seems to happen.

Enter Village Elder 2

Village Elder 1.
What are those footsteps behind me? Identify
yourself? Oh, it's you. Well, come along with me
then. I think I have found our village leader, Dorado.

Village Elder 2.
I can hear singing and chanting coming from ahead,
and it sounds like some satanic ritual.

Chorus.
(*singing*)
He will not survive. He will not survive. Because he
will be caught. The Village Elders are coming after
him. His secret will be found out. He is a witch, a
witch, a witch. Oh No, what's that? He is flying on a
broom. He has a black pointy hat he is wearing. He is
a witch doctor and he will be found out before doing
any more harm. He is a goner, a goner, and he shall
die tonight. He shall not survive.

Narrator.
The two Village Elders finds Dorado and they are
shocked to see what he is doing.

Village Elder 1.
What have we here, practicing witchcraft I see?

Village Elder 2.
You are dead to the tribe of El Dorado and you shall
be executed for your crimes. We don't care if you
founded this tribe. You will not ruin this for us,
because you are engaging in some satanic ritual that is
evil.

Narrator.

The two Village Elders grab Dorado and tie his hands, arms, and feet together so he can't escape. Dorado won't be escaping anytime soon, because he will soon be executed. He has been found out and will suffer the consequences.

Chorus.
(*singing*)

The time is now. The time is soon. He has been caught. He has been captured. He shall be executed. He shall receive justice for his actions. He won't survive. He will die. He shall die. He let everyone down. People will kill him. Dorado won't be alive anymore and he won't be able to do anything about it. There is just something no one can do. Something is going down and it will be the end of the reign. No one will be able to escape the wrath of Dorado.

[Exeunt All]

SCENE 4. El Dorado, North America. 1354
Town Square.

Enter Magistrate of the Court and Dorado

Magistrate of the Court.

Dorado, our dear leader of the tribe, which is also named after you, you are hereby accused of practicing witchcraft. How do you plead?

Dorado.

Your honor, as your friend, I plead not guilty. Practicing witchcraft is not against the law. It is not illegal. It is not a problem to practice witchcraft.

Magistrate of the Court.
After further consideration, I have found you guilty of your crimes, because committing witchcraft is an immoral and very dangerous act. I don't if witchcraft is legal. You were engaged in an immoral act that destroys the history of morality, and therefore you are found guilty. You shall be executed today, in a few minutes, and you will never harm people with your so-called practice of witchcraft ever again.

[Exeunt Magistrate of the Court]

Enter Narrator

Narrator.
Dorado is taken to a tree nearby, about a minute's walk away, and still in the town square. Someone ties a rope around his neck and then lifts him up on top of a platform so that he can be killed once the platform doors open below him, which will kill him instantly once the box falls down.

Dorado.
In the name of my ancestors and of my religion, I put a curse on you and all who set foot on my land forever and eternity. I will haunt you for the rest of your lives and for eternity. All of your descendants shall be cursed as well. No one shall be immune from my curse. All of you shall die a horrible death and no one shall know what it will be, because everyone shall be dead one-by-one. And then suddenly, many people will die at once.

[Exeunt Dorado]

Narrator.

No one cared what Dorado said. After he spoke for the last time, the lever was pulled and Dorado died instantly. All of the village people moved on without Dorado and no one cared about him anymore. But after Dorado was hanged for his crimes of immorality the entire tribe of El Dorado experienced something drastic and dire. People started to die and soon the entire village died. Everything else soon died and the tribe died off, like it never existed at all.

[Exeunt All]

ACT II

SCENE 1. Ashford, Connecticut. 1705 - 1941
Woods

Enter Narrator

Narrator.
By 1705, the once vibrant El Dorado is changed to
Ashford. Ever since Dorado was killed that day, the
entire tribe vanished, and everything was
undeveloped, but now, since 1705, prominent people
from the world started to remove overgrown trees,
bushes, and other foliage.

Enter Lumberjack 1

Lumberjack 1.
Go set forth and destroy this land to build more
homes.

Enter Lumberjack 2 and Lumberjack 3

Lumberjack 2.
(singing)
I am a lumberjack. I chop down trees, chop down
trees. I destroy the forest, destroy the forest. I do this
to help my family. I don't like the woods. They scare
me. Trees should be outlawed because they could kill
you. Anything could be hiding in there. I am a
lumberjack. I chop down trees, chop down trees. I
destroy the forest, destroy the forest. I don't care
about anything but me and my family. I will destroy
the forest because it needs to be done.

Lumberjack 3.
Chop that wood, chop that wood. We need to build
homes for the rich people. We need to chop down
everything we see. No tree must remain standing.
Everything must be torn down. It is not a travesty. It is
the way it must be. Nothing is sacred because
everything is worthless. Everything must be destroyed
in order to make room for the new. It is just how life
works. All must be replaced. People must have a place
to live. It is how life shall be for the rest of the life.
People are idiots and they will never act alone. It is
always a sham and people will make an attempt to
destroy what they love the most. Nothing is safe from
anything because they are the real destructive forces
of history.

Lumber Jack 2.
Chopping wood is good. It is part of life. It is we get
paid. We must make sure every settler has a place to
live. All new people from different countries have
paid good money in order to live in a new home. It is
just like it is. Nothing shall remain. It is just that part
of life.

Narrator.
The lumberjacks kept on chopping down the trees
with their axes and saws. It was a workout for them
but they enjoyed the sweat on their faces and rest of
their body because they knew they were working hard
and accomplishing something that would benefit the
future of society.

Lumberjack 1.
It is time for a new society. People will be moving
here soon. We must be prepared. We need to be ready.

It is just that time again, and again, to continue the way of life. People are people. It is just the way of life. No one can escape. Others are on the brink of a new freedom. It is the reason why people are people but there is nothing but the rest of society.

Lumberjack 3.
It will take months to tear down these trees. Good for us but bad for the rest of people who want a new place to live. We get paid by the tree per hour and we own our own company. It is just how it works and it must remain the same. People are the same and they shall be the same as they were always. It is just that fact of life.

Lumberjack 2.
Move, move! Go to your positions. Attack the trees with your axes and saws. It is time to tear down all of these trees once and for all. It is time and it shall continue. Our charter has been granted from the British government. It is time for everyone to accept the consequences of chopping down these trees because it is necessary to live.

Lumberjack 3.
These trees are in our way. We chop and saw one at a time, each. It is easy but never gets old. It is just part of life and it must get to the rage of society.

Lumberjack1.
We are not done yet. There is still some more to do. It will take a while but we should be done within a month. Then people can finally arrive here and view the land. People can build houses now and that is all that is needed. People must take their time and it is

about the time and place to enter. It is their chance to survive in the colony of Connecticut. People are people and they want and need a place to live. It is just their way of showing respect to the rest of life.

Lumberjack 3.
We chop down more trees. We chop down more trees. We need to remove the stumps of each tree. We need more tools once we finish the job of chopping and sawing down all of these trees. It is just the way of life.

Lumberjack 2.
It is time. It is time. People need to build homes. They need to find a place to live. It is about life and it is about the way of the future. It is how life was meant to be. There is a time to be a crazy person but it is about the right of the time. No one is about the time to call to the uprisings. There are people waiting for new houses to be built. Everything should be ready in a matter of a few weeks. It is about time and it is ready to understand that there is time to know about everything.

Lumberjack 1.
We are almost finished. The land should be ready for new construction in a short amount of time. There is no time to lose because everything is money. No one wants to waste a bunch of time. Money is time and time costs money. Everything needs to be completed on schedule. There is just a case for the rest of the future. It is just how it was meant to be. It is about time and money so people should buckle up and get ready for the ride because everything is about to change.

Narrator.
After a month, the lumberjacks have completed the job of chopping and sawing down all of the trees as well as removing all tree stumps. The land is now completely vacant and it looks as beautiful as ever. It is such a lush green landscape that looks as though it belongs to a tribe of Leprechauns from Ireland. It is such a beautiful landscape that people should be aware of it. There is such the tone of everything that must be said. No one can escape that and it shall be forever that. People will start acting in a new place of manner but it is now has been completed.

Lumberjack 3.
All is done.

Lumberjack 1.
Everything looks like it is brand new.

Lumberjack 2.
It looks beautiful.

Lumberjack 1.
It was a job well done.

Enter Lumberjack 4 and Lumberjack 5

Lumberjack 4.
It is time to plan for the construction of new houses.

Lumberjack 5.
We not only cut down trees but we also build houses.

Lumberjack 3.
Let's begin building those houses. All shall be made

of wood and shall include stone and brick components as well. The roofs shall be made out of wood, and there shall be a concrete foundation. Each house shall have a cellar and an attic. And there shall be stone or brick frames and walls that are reinforced with wood and wooden beams/ It is how it is meant to be. We have time and we shall build houses. But there shall also be a fireplace and chimney to warm the houses during the cold months of the year. It is life and it is now.

Narrator.
The lumberjacks start building the houses one-by-one and it takes them about a month or so to complete each new building. The houses are big but not that small.

Lumberjack 5.
Let us build, build, build, build, build. We build houses. We will make room for the rest of the new people. We will go to the ends of the earth to make sure people have a place to live. It is that reason for why we need to help the new settlers. This is the colony of Connecticut, Connecticut. We are the future of the British Empire. We need to conquer, we need to stand together. and we need to make sure everything is in place. We build, let us build, build, build, build, built. We build houses. We will make room for the rest of the new people. This is the colony of Connecticut.

Lumberjack 2.
Through the edges of the green grass. We find something new, and something that is now at hand. We need to make sure that something is at the time

and place of everything. It is the reason why everything is at the place of a decision. It is why everything has a meaning. We will build until we die. It is for that purpose we stand together no matter how long it takes. We are building houses and we will make sure they are proper and what will make a place for a new home. It is the reason why we live in order to make sure we are the best in the world.

Narrator.
The lumberjacks have been working hard building the houses for the new people. New settlers from all over the world have moved in after construction was completed. It is still the year 1705 but only twenty-nine houses were built because that is how much space was allotted, but there could be more built yet that would give less space to each new settler. In order to build such many houses in a new neighborhood, the lumberjacks brought in a crew of over five-hundred other laborers and lumberjacks so that the project can be finished before the end of the year. And it was a success, since everything was completed five months ahead of schedule. But no one knows what will happen next. It could be the news of the century.

Enter Chorus

Chorus.
(*singing*)
The colony of Connecticut, Connecticut, is going to hell. People are in for a surprise. They won't know anything and they won't even know that they are in grave danger. There are evil forces out to get the new settlers. It is the price they will all have to pay. It is for that why there must be the reason why people are

crazy. They are just going to die. All of the colony of Connecticut will die and it will be when they fail to notice anything.

[Exeunt All But Narrator]

Narrator.
In 1745, the original settlers and the lumberjacks as well as the other members of the construction team from 1705 have died, due to small pox, the Black Plague, and pneumonia.

By 1753, more people arrived from England, Spain, and France, and they start to develop the town of Ashford, Connecticut even further.

In 1758, the new settlers from England, Spain, and France finally finished developing the old dirt roads into real concrete roads of what used to be clay sand and filled with trees and bushes. Everything is entering a new chapter, and people will settle for the better of their lives.

By 1761, there is a drought, followed by a bitter and caustic snowstorm. Everyone dies, and soon, the project remains abandoned.

In 1850 more people start to arrive after a near century of almost forgetting about a small and impossible town. In a little over a year, the new people have settled in, and houses start to appear all over town. It is quite simple, and the time is growing in a vibrant economy, filled with shenanigans and upheaval in government structure. There is one part that is not developed, a spot of land that is fifty acres. Near the cemetery, it will soon change.

By 1875, developers start to develop this useful plot of land, and they knock down everything with saws and other equipment. Across the area, there is a sense of reactions, towards the vital sequence of undated material. People have no clue about what is going on, but they continue to open their mind, rather than develop a harsher meaning. Folklore is clear, but is it real. The precise cause for the nonsense of everything is the direct threat to humanity.

Around the year 1895, the land is fully developed, and the construction of the house has begun. Normally there will be a neighborhood filled with multiple units, but the developer only wants to build one house, and he gets what he wants. He turns the land into a wonderful landscape, filled with gardens and grass, and a small farm. Construction begins and it takes one year to complete, and by now, there is some sort of expensive quality of life. For months, no one buys the house, and for years, the same thing happens.

But on 1941, we come to the true story now, about a family, who finally bought the house, of what used to be Dorado's land. No one actually knew why anyone bought the house. The developers were amazed, because it was a classic, and it was about nothing. People say that the house was haunted because it was on the site of an Indian burial ground, and then there were others who said it was cursed, but did Dorado really exist.

[Exeunt All]

SCENE 2. **Ashford, Connecticut. 1941**
Plantation

Enter Narrator

Narrator.
A family moves into the abandoned property. The
family was made up about five people the parents and
three teenaged children, a boy and two girls. The
father's name was John, and he was married to
Christine. Their children were Danielle, 18, Catherine,
19, and Robert, 16. It was quite the family, because
everything was normal and everything seemed
normal, but that is going to change in the near future.
John was 42 and Christine was 41, and both of them
lived happily, or so you think.

During one night, there was an incident, an incident
on the farm area. On a dark and stormy night, there
was an incident on the farm, near the apple tree, but
what happened next would only startle you.

Danielle, the eldest daughter, met a boy, by the name
of Larry, and on that night, they made love, in the
cornfield.

You see, Danielle just turned eighteen a day ago, and
she was no stranger to sex, so she found a willing
participant that wanted to have sex, but that night, it
would turn ugly. Danielle and Larry started to make
out which ultimately led to making love. But, when
they were done making love, Danielle went missing,
which could mean something sinister.

Danielle was such a manipulator that no one could

escape her grasp. It was such a thing only an expert could undertake. Danielle was such a master at using manipulation that no one could escape her. She is the enemy and should be held accountable.

[Exeunt Narrator]

Enter Danielle and Larry

Danielle.
Hello, what is your name?

Larry.
My name is Lawrence Ashman Wilmington, but you and everyone else can call me Larry.

Danielle.
Such an extravagant name! Are you royalty?

Larry.
No. I am just a drifter who moves from place to place for work.

Danielle.
Hmm, that's interesting and quite intriguing. I like that in a man.

Larry.
Thank you! I do what I have to get by.

Danielle.
You wanna make out?

Larry.
That is a fine idea. Yes, I do.

Danielle.
Take off your shirt. I want to see your muscles.

Larry.
Okay then.

Danielle.
Is there anything wrong?

Larry.
No. No one has admired my muscles or body before.

Danielle.
Well, I will be the first.

Enter Narrator

Narrator.
Larry takes off his shirt and then Danielle slowly places her hand on his muscles so that she can feel them. One thing leads to another and Danielle starts to embrace Larry and then she kisses Larry passionately in a way of love. Then that leads to Danielle and Larry tearing off each other's clothes and they begin making love with each other on the ground of the plantation.

Danielle.
Take me now.

Larry.
Okay then.

Danielle.
Make love to me now.

Narrator.
After a while, Danielle and Larry stop making love,
and they each go their separate ways, but something
happens after they have left. Danielle went missing.
What happens next was a loud scream, followed by
another loud scream, which would later develop into
something further, something more dramatic, but
what.

[Exeunt Danielle and Larry]

Enter Catherine

Catherine.
(Shouting to anyone outside)
Has anyone seen my sister, Danielle?

Narrator.
Catherine went looking for Danielle, and found her
body hanging in the barn, naked, with blood. She was
shocked at what she found. Catherine did not know
what to do and she believed she could be the next
victim. You might think Catherine was startled, but
she didn't scream, and then Robert went looking for
Catherine and Danielle. It is possible that Catherine
could be the killer because she was not startled. By the
morning, John and Christine went looking for their
children, because no one ever came home.

[Exeunt Catherine]

Enter Robert

Robert.
Hello, is anyone there? I am looking for my sisters,

Catherine and Danielle.

Narrator.
John and Christine, the parents of Danielle, Christine, and Robert begin looking for Danielle.

Enter John and Christine

John.
Has anyone my daughters, Danielle and Catherine?

Christine.
Hello, is anyone out there? Can you hear me? I am looking for my daughters, Danielle and Catherine.

John.
Hello, anyone there?

Christine.
Let's split up. I will check around the cornfields.

John.
I will check the house and the barn.

Christine.
I will tell you if I found her.

Narrator.
John and Christine have been searching for hours and hours. Morning has passed and it was almost afternoon.

Robert.
Hello, is anyone still here? Where the hell am I?

Narrator.
Robert did not know where he was. In fact, he was still on the plantation, but he was in some sort of man-made maze.

Robert.
I think I'm going in the same direction over and over again.

[Exeunt Robert]

Narrator.
Later that afternoon, John found Danielle hanging naked in the barn, and developed depression. Blood was dripping everywhere. It was like a horror film, but only worse. The blood trickled down the ceiling onto John's clothing, and it landed on his face. Quickly, John tried to run away, but it was too late, and now he was stuck. The barn door banged shut, and a breeze started to gain entrance.

The breeze took over John's body and made him feel depressed. John couldn't stand seeing his daughter being dead, and so, he committed suicide, because of what had happened.

Catherine was nowhere to be found, and the same was for Larry, but Robert was missing. Christine soon looked for everyone, but got lost in the cornfield, but she soon found the barn and went inside, but to find John and Danielle dead.

Christine was shocked to find that two members of the family were dead, and she started to break down in tears, but something happened.

Nobody knew what was happening. At the very sight that something was happening, there would be a breeze in the air, and that would later mysteriously disappear.

The whole concept was there was someone that existed, and that someone did not want anyone to be on his or her former land.

A scarecrow appeared and it started to stare at people. No one ever saw that scarecrow before, and it wasn't on the property before, so it would have to be a coincidence.

Someone was behind Christine, but whom? Well whoever it was, Christine didn't see anything coming. Christine started to scream, and moaned, and she finally stops breathing. Christine was no longer alive, because she was killed, but by who, and the answer might surprise you.

Catherine killed her mother, Christine, because Catherine wanted to, and it was all part of her plan all along. Catherine was completely naked at the time of the killing, because that was the best possible option, so that all possible evidence could be destroyed, as Catherine believed she could wash off the blood immediately.

[Exeunt All]

SCENE 3. Ashford, Connecticut. 1941
Inside Barn of Plantation

Enter Narrator

Narrator.
Catherine already graduated from college a month ago, because Catherine was also very smart for her age.

Catherine graduated high school at the age of fourteen, with honors, and she was only accepted to Yale, because that is the only place where she applied, and she was offered a spot immediately. She was so smart that the initial essay and interview were not required. Catherine was enrolled as a dual major, with an emphasis in biology and another in chemistry, and this took one year longer. So, the initial cause was that she is extremely intelligent, but why would she start killing her family.

Later that night, Larry went missing, and Robert was nowhere to be found.

Enter Larry and Robert

Larry.
Who are you?

Robert.
My name is Robert, and I live on this plantation.

Larry.
Are you related to Danielle and Catherine?

Robert.
Yes

Larry.
Well, they have gone missing and I am looking for them. Now that I've found you, I will see if I can find your sisters.

Robert.
I will see you later.

[Exeunt Robert]

Enter Catherine

Catherine.
Is anyone there? I am looking for my sister.

Larry.
Hello, Catherine, your brother just left the barn and is headed to find your sister.

Catherine.
Okay then, I will be going home now. I will resume the search in the morning.

Narrator.
Larry goes deeper into the barn but fails to find the bodies. Meanwhile, Catherine pretends to exit the barn. She then undresses herself in order to not get any evidence on her.

Catherine.
That was a relief. I feel better now after taking off all of my clothes.

Narrator.
Larry claims he can hear footsteps, but he looks behind him and sees nothing every time he looks back at what he thinks might be making the noise. But, Catherine is quietly hiding behind the hay with an axe in hand waiting to attack Larry because Larry knows something.

Larry.
What are you doing with that axe and why are you naked? Do you want to make love again?

Catherine.
Yes, I do want to make love again. Take off your clothes now. The axe is to cut wood for a camp fire tomorrow.

Narrator.
While Larry takes off his clothes so he can make love to Catherine, Catherine decides to use the axe against Larry.

Catherine.
Die, you piece of shit. You have been a burden on me the day we met. You won't ruin this for me ever. I will make sure you are dead before I get caught. I will always be above the law and shall flee justice in order to evade justice. Nobody will believe anything you say because you will be dead. I will destroy any and all evidence and I will not be arrested.

Narrator.
Larry felt something, behind his back. Some type of breeze touched him. Larry turned around and looked to his surprise and disbelief.

Larry.
What are you doing?

Catherine.
I am killing you with my axe you piece of shit. I don't care about you. I just wanted to use you.

Larry.
You won't get away with this.

Catherine.
I already have gotten away with it.

Narrator.
It was too late. Catherine killed Larry with the same axe as she did with Danielle and Christine. Since Larry was now dead, Catherine must find a way to dispose of her clothes and of the evidence linking her to the crimes she committed.

[Exeunt Larry]

Enter Robert

Robert.
What are you doing here, and why are you naked?

Catherine.
This concerns none of your business.

Robert.
I'm telling mother and father.

Catherine.
It's too late for that you sick jerk. I killed mom and
Danielle. Father killed himself after finding Danielle
hanging. I was here the whole time and I saw
everything. And you are next.

Robert.
I'm calling the police.

Catherine.
Oh no you're not, I'm going to kill you now.

Narrator.
Catherine kills her brother, Robert. She continues to
whack Robert until he falls to the ground and has no
pulse whatsoever. It takes three minutes for Catherine
to kill Robert.

[Exeunt Robert]

Catherine.
Now to go back to the house to clean up and to get
some things.

Narrator.
Catherine goes back into the house in order to wash
up and to pack her stuff because she was going to
leave soon. You might say that this is impossible, but
this part of land is still in a secluded area, but it is also
private property, bought by a wealthy family. Yet, it is
still unknown when she is going to leave. She might
leave in the early morning or sometime tonight. It is

just something that she needs to think about. But if she thinks about leaving tonight it will be in a few short hours. Otherwise, Catherine will have a chance to do something better.

[Exeunt All]

SCENE 4. Ashford, Connecticut. 1941
Plantation (House and Barn)

Enter Catherine and Narrator

Catherine.
What to do now? I know, I shall take a shower in order to get rid of any evidence.

Narrator.
Catherine takes a shower to get rid of any and all evidence.

Catherine.
I think that is all of the blood and dirt, but I don't feel like getting dressed yet. I feel like something more needs to be done.

Narrator.
Catherine is finished with her shower and she packs her clothes in her suitcases so she can be ready when she needs to leave. Catherine then proceeds to walk outside naked in order to destroy the barn.

Catherine.
Off to the barn I go, where I will burn it down in order to destroy the evidence.

Narrator.
Catherine arrives at the barn, where all of the dead bodies are. But she decides to go to the garage near the house in order to gather ten packs of C4 plastic explosives, a timer, a fifty-foot ignition wire, and a remote.

Catherine.
I forgot, I need to go to the garage first in order to get ten packs of C4 plastic explosives, a timer, a fifty-foot ignition wire, and a remote.

Narrator.
Catherine retrieves the supplies and heads back to the barn.

Catherine.
Great, time to get this done!

Narrator.
Catherine arrives back at the barn and finally sets up the explosives, and then she goes back to the garage where she gets ten grenades.

Catherine.
Dammit, I forgot to get grenades. I guess I have to go back to the garage again.

Narrator.
Catherine arrives back at the garage and grabs ten grenades.

Catherine.
Now, back to the barn in order to burn the bodies and the evidence

Narrator.
Catherine leaves the garage with the grenades and arrives back at the garage after eight minutes. Now is the easy part for her, blowing up the barn.

Catherine.
Time to blow up and destroy the barn in order to get rid of the evidence.

Narrator.
Catherine places the grenades in the dirt, hiding them, and then she realizes she has to take another shower to remove the dirt again.

Catherine.
Damnit, I need to take another shower. Oh Well!

Narrator.
Catherine arrives back at the house and takes a shower again in order to remove more dirt. After the shower, Catherine gets dressed, but does not put on too many clothes because she doesn't want to feel too exhausted if the weather gets too hot.

Catherine.
Time to get ready and to head to the local airport and then to push the remote after I am at a safe distance away. Now, to head to the car.

Narrator.
Catherine grabs her suitcases and the remote and takes them to the car, a 1935 Rolls Royce. She places the suitcases in the trunk and the remote in the front passenger seat.

Catherine.
Finally, I can leave, since I put everything in the car or trunk as needed.

Narrator.
After everything is in the car, Catherine drives off and heads to the airport in Connecticut, where she will leave and go to Moscow.

Catherine.
I see the gate straight ahead. Now, where did I place that remote?

Narrator.
Catherine finds the remote and she holds onto it with her right hand.

Catherine.
Finally, I have exited the gate and am now on the road to the local airport. Time to push that button on that remote I'm holding.

Narrator.
After Catherine exits the road from the gate, she pushes the button on the remote and heads for the airport.

Catherine.
The explosion was successful. Now to the airport

[Exeunt All]

SCENE 4. Ashford, Connecticut. 1941
Airport and Plantation

Enter Narrator and Catherine

Narrator.
Catherine arrives at the airport and parks it in a
secluded area. After she is inside the airport, she
reaches in her pants pocket and presses a button, and
this time to blow up the car.

Catherine.
Perfect, the plan went according to plan. Now, I am
safely away from my car and am inside the airport,
where I will now go to Russia.

Narrator.
After an hour passed, she boarded her plane, and it
took off in less than an hour, but before that, she put
both remotes in the garbage. It was about ten o'clock
in the evening, and the flight departed. Eight hours
later the plane landed and she bought an apartment
with money she brought from home, but exchanged it
to Russian money at the airport.

[Exeunt Catherine]

Enter Concerned Citizen

Concerned Citizen.
Oh, My? I need to call the police because I see
something burning nearby my house. I need to call the
police before my property gets caught on fire as well.
I will not die tonight.

Narrator.
The concerned citizen calls the police to warn them
that something near her is on fire.

Concerned Citizen.
Hello, police, I believe the property next to me is on
fire. Hurry. I am next to the old plantation near Ash
Road.

Enter Police Dispatcher

Police Dispatcher.
We will send someone over there now. If you think
you feel unsafe try to go somewhere where you are far
away from any fire.

[Exeunt Police Dispatcher]

Enter Police Deputy

Police Deputy.
Oh, my! Everything is burning.

Narrator.
By the next morning, the fire died down and nothing
was in flames anymore. The police searched and
searched but could not find anything, so the case was
closed.

[Exeunt All]

ACT III

SCENE 1. Ashford, Connecticut. 1968
Plantation

Enter Narrator

Narrator.
The year is now October of 1968, where a family has
bought the house. Everything is fine at first, but their
German Shepherd, by the name of Ivan, refuses to
enter the house and chooses to stay outside.

Later that night, it rains, and Ivan gets scared, and
barks at the door, but no one hears him. In the course
of events, everyone goes to sleep, and everyone is in
bed now. The entire family never heard Ivan because
the house was sound proof.

In the morning afterwards, the family wakes up, and
everyone is awake now.

Enter Abigail and Cynthia

Abigail.
Oh My God! Oh My God! What has happened? Oh
My God!

Narrator.
Abigail sees Ivan chopped up and mutilated into
several pieces with organs showing, and flies buzzing
around. She runs screaming into her bedroom and
shuts the door behind her.

Cynthia.
Oh My God! What happened? Ahhhhhhhh! I don't feel that good.

Narrator.
Cynthia is so horrified at what she saw that she collapses right next to the deceased remains of Ivan, the family dog.

Abigail.
Mom, Dad, look what happened to Ivan!

Narrator.
Everyone is shocked at what they see. Lindsay, the mother of Abigail and Cynthia, digs a hole for Ivan's corpse, since everything else is just a pile of blood and organs. Only the skeleton of Ivan is buried, and since the fur is contaminated with blood, nobody wants to pick it up. Peter, the father, calls the police, so that the death can be investigated.

[Exeunt Abigail and Cynthia]

Enter Peter

Peter.
Hello, police, I would like to report a mysterious death. Our family dog died and it seems all of his organs exploded. There is blood everywhere. We live on the big plantation.

Police Dispatcher

Police Dispatcher.
We will send someone soon.

Narrator.
The police sends over someone by the name of
William Ash, who is a detective, sergeant, lieutenant,
and is in charge of local operations.

[Exeunt Police Dispatcher and Narrator]

Enter William Ash

William Ash.
What seems to be the problem here?

Peter.
Our family dog died of a mysterious illness. We
buried the skeleton, as it was separated from the rest
of the body. All other remains of our family dog is
right in front of you. All that remains is the fur, blood,
and organs.

William Ash.
I believe I have seen this before or at least heard of
other occurrences that might apply to this situation of
yours.

Peter.
So you think you know what killed our family dog?

William Ash.
Yes, and there is a story that goes along with it, which
is as follows:

During the fourteenth century, there was a legend
about a tribe, a tribe that was home to the lost city of
El Dorado. There was a story that the tribe found out
that their leader, Dorado, the founder of the tribe was

practicing witchcraft without their knowledge. Dorado was immediately hanged and he died, but before he stood silent, he cursed everyone who built on his land. He cursed anyone who step foot on his land, and he cursed anyone who lived on it. He finally became silent, but after that day, all members of the tribe were never seen again.

As we fast forward together, a family bought the house in 1941, but there was a strange occurrence. Legend says that the oldest daughter, Catherine, murdered her sister, her brother, her parents, and her sister's boyfriend, and blew up the barn with grenades and demolition devices, such as C4 plastic explosives. It also tells that she was completely naked when killing everyone, and that after she finished the murders, she took her parents car, a Rolls Royce and took it the airport, where she blew it up in a secluded area, and then hopped on a plane to Moscow to Russia.

For now, you could say that this land is haunted, but people have complained about hearing voices, voices that sound like they are from the dead or the devil himself. No one actually knows what happened, but there has been a report that Catherine committed suicide in Russia because she wanted to feel pain.

Peter.
So you are saying our dog was killed by a curse by some witch doctor?

William Ash.
I never did say that. No one really believes that story about Dorado, as all believe it is just a myth and some

fable to scare children. But, people can decide for themselves.

Peter.
Well, what do you think killed our dog?

William Ash.
As for your dog, there has also been the report of a wild serial killer, known only to man as the ghost nymph. People hardly see the ghost nymph, but there were some people on our police force that saw it, and they remembered it distinctively. The ghost nymph, as some of our deputies recalled, resembled a young twenty year old, according to age descriptions. The ghost nymph seemed not to be wearing any clothes and had in her hand was an axe and a dagger, combined into one. There was one piece of clothing she had, but it was only around her neck, which was a scarf.

Peter.
Are you saying the thing or person that killed our dog is a deceased person haunting the land.

William Ash.
Possibly! It could be the ghost of Catherine.

Peter.
That doesn't make any sense at all.

William Ash.
The supernatural can do things that might surprise you. Don't expect everything to be safe, because your land could be haunted by evil forces.

Peter.
What are you going to do with the pile of blood and organs?

William Ash.
I will take samples of the blood, organs, and fur as evidence before I leave.

Peter.
Anything else we should know?

William Ash.
Yes.

Peter.
Do you think you know what caused this?

William Ash.
Possibly. From this distance, which I stand now, I think your dog was possessed and then killed, which he died from explosive humiliation.

Peter.
Explosive humiliation? What exactly is that?

William Ash.
It might sound strange but it can happen. There have also been many reports that since this land has been vacated for over twenty years that teenagers reported having sex, but that they kept hearing voices inside their head, yet that is not the point. The point about the teenagers is when they had sex in the cornfield they felt they were being humiliated because they heard a voice telling their personal secrets out of nowhere. After a few days passed, it was also reported

that some of those teenagers died, but when the autopsy was completed for each of them, it revealed that the cause of death was organ failure, because all organs were liquefied.

Peter.
That is very strange.

William Ash.
Your family dog seems to had his organs almost liquefied, because as I am feeling them right now they are extremely soft and weak.

Peter.
How long will it take to examine the samples?

William Ash.
A few days. We are lucky to have one of the best state of the art crime labs in our police department.

Peter.
Anything else I should know?

William Ash.
This land is some mystery but it does have a history of scaring and scarring people for life. If I were you, I would hire paranormal investigators. Something bad could happen any day now, and it could be worse than what happened to your dog. I have been with the force since 1923, and I can tell you, from my experience, that I have seen everything, from minor itches to major crimes. I am almost sixty-seven years old and I have been with the force for forty-five years. Things change and when I retire I will l leave immediately. If you need me, I will be at the police station. Good luck

with your new home, and I hope you find Ashford appealing to you.

Peter.
See you later.

Enter Narrator

Narrator.
With that, the old police detective left the residence with some samples as evidence, and he vanished out of thin air. No one knew him quite well, but he sure does know a lot about the history of this land. He might be connected to it, or he might as well be something else.

Everything could be a coincidence, but something always happens in the end. There is some sort of saying, but it could lead it up to the mystery that lies beneath the soil. Without a trace, a time was instilled, and forever, there stood a hole in the environment. Some say that it was a ghost, but others say it was a miracle. There is just too much to find out, and many times people will figure a way to promote the cause of good hope.

Peter.
Now it is time to bury the dog. Hopefully, something like this won't happen again.

Narrator.
Peter buried the remaining parts of the dog while everyone else watched in disbelief. Some were crying while others wanted to look away. It was just a sad state of affairs.

Peter.
Everyone back in the house now. I need to decontaminate myself from all of this blood. It is such a sad day.

Narrator.
Everyone went back inside the house.

[Exeunt All]

SCENE 2 Ashford, Connecticut. 1968
Plantation House

Enter Narrator

Narrator.
Ivan was buried that afternoon. It took three hours to bury the rest of the remains of Ivan. It was surely a sad day.

Enter Peter

Peter.
What's that noise? Anyone there?

Narrator.
Peter decides to get up and explore.

Peter.
Hello, if anyone is there, I have a gun and am not afraid to use it. Be warned.

Narrator.
But, there is an unexpected surprise. Lindsay wakes up for a few seconds to ask what is going on.

Enter Lindsay

Lindsay.
Who are you talking to?

Peter.
I thought I heard some noises.

Lindsay.
Noises from where?

Peter.
I don't know. I think it is just the wind. But I want to make sure it is nothing sinister.

Lindsay.
Just be safe. And try not to wake up the kids.

Peter.
I will see you when I see you.

Lindsay.
Just try to be safe. I love you! Good luck!

Narrator.
With that, Peter left the bedroom and went looking for what was making the noises he heard.

Peter.
Is anyone there? Show yourself now and you will be fine. I have a gun and am not afraid to use it. If you don't show yourself I will be prepared to shoot you, so don't be afraid. If anyone is here I want to know if you hear me. This is your last chance.

Narrator.
Peter is approaching the hallway and he still hears the noises. But it is just the wind and trees. Peter can't see anything that looks suspicious.

Peter.
Hello, I am nearing the kitchen now. If you are there prepare to show yourself.

Narrator.
And then the cupboards and cabinets in the kitchen start to making noise. It is such a racket that Peter races to wonder what it is.

Peter.
Show yourself now or be warned.

Narrator.
Then there were loud screams as Peter approached the kitchen and he raced there to see what has happened, or so he thought.

Peter.
I am in the kitchen now. Are you here? Where are you? I demand you show yourself.

Narrator.
Peter opened up a cupboard and saw nothing out of the ordinary, but he did not see the ghost nymph looking at him.

Peter.
Well, that was a bummer. I thought I heard someone or something screaming. It was probably something else. Oh Well, back to bed now.

Narrator.
Peter goes back to bed after arriving back at the master bedroom.

Lindsay.
Find anything?

Peter.
No, but I heard noises.

Lindsay.
Must be the wind then.

Peter.
I thought I heard someone screaming.

Lindsay.
Funny you say that, I didn't hear anything.

Peter.
Must be the wind howling again.

Narrator.
It is the next day and Lindsay wakes up to find something disturbing. Her husband's eyes are wide open but he shows no sign of movement. Peter is just looking up at the ceiling. Lindsay decides to call the police requesting an ambulance.

[Exeunt Peter]

Lindsay.
Hello, police, I need an ambulance. My husband can't move. His eyes are wide open.

Enter Police Dispatcher

Police Dispatcher.
Do you need the police or just an ambulance?

Lindsay.
Just the ambulance. I don't know what happened to
my husband.

Police Dispatcher.
Where do you live ma'am?

Lindsay.
By the old plantation house.

Police Dispatcher.
We will send someone there to assess the situation
along with the ambulance.

Narrator.
The ambulance arrives and the paramedics sees that
Peter is in a trance for an unknown reason. The two
paramedics place Peter on a stretcher and take him
back to the ambulance so that he can be assessed at
the hospital.

[Exeunt All]

SCENE 3. Ashford, Connecticut. 1968.
Hospital

Enter William Ash

William Ash.
What do we have here?

Enter Doctor and Nurse

Doctor.
It seems something has happened. Have we notified the next of kin?

Nurse.
Not yet. They should be notified in a few minutes.

Doctor.
Good. Someone needs to find out what happened. We need to conduct some tests before any family or friends arrive.

Nurse.
There must be something that will allow us to know why this happened.

Doctor.
This looks certainly unusual. I have never seen this before.

Nurse.
When he came in it looked like he was in a trance.

Doctor.
A trance might explain why he wasn't moving. It resembled a comatose yet vegetative state. This is very unusual.

Nurse.
Very unusual.

Doctor.
I can understand something like a trance but not something like this.

Nurse.
Something doesn't seem right here.

William Ash.
I have contacted the next of kin. They should be here shortly.

Doctor.
Thank you Dr. Ash

William Ash.
Where any of you here when this happened?

Doctor.
No

Nurse.
No

Doctor.
I just heard some sort of explosion

Nurse.
I was walking down the hall and heard a loud noise.

William Ash.
Hmm, this seems familiar and interesting.

Doctor.
What do you mean?

William Ash.
I have seen this before.

Doctor.
From where.

William Ash.
The other day I received a call from the deceased about their dog. It seemed the family dog died of something mysterious. All of the organs were splattered everywhere with a big pile of blood. It seemed the organs were soft. The fur was covered with blood and something that resembled acid. They already buried the skeleton but the family just wanted to know what happened to their dog. I believed the dog died from explosive humiliation because of what has happened.

Nurse.
Oh My.

Doctor.
That seems very strange. I have never heard of that ever before.

Nurse.
Very strange indeed.

William Ash.
Yes, indeed very strange. I suspect the same thing happened to our deceased patient here. He first went into a trance by the ghost nymph followed by death via explosive humiliation. I don't know how it works but I believe the explosive humiliation is based on an internal mechanism that makes the body explode into pieces after a certain amount of time.

Doctor.
Any idea how long it will take the family to get here?

William Ash.
Probably about ten minutes. They are living in a rural part of the city with dirt roads.

Nurse.
So, how do we clean up this mess?

William Ash.
We should preserve as much as we can. We should collect several samples by placing anything we can in a number of vials. We need to autopsy any of the organs in order to see what happened. And we need to clean up this mess after we have collected all of the samples and placed them in vials and placed the organs in necessary evidence bags. This hospital room needs to undergo a very deep cleaning because it could lead to possible contamination of people getting infected.

Doctor.
Sounds reasonable. When do we start all of that?

William Ash.
When the family arrives.

Nurse.
I hear footsteps.

William Ash.
It seems like the family has arrived.

Doctor.
Should we allow them in the room.

William Ash.
Probably, but for safety precautions, you should decontaminate yourself in the hospital showers, as a way to avoid infecting other people.

Nurse.
How about me?

William Ash.
I advise you to do the same. Besides, I need to speak with the family first because I know more about what probably happened to their deceased family member. They might feel less stressed out because they don't know that I am also the medical examiner.

Doctor.
Alright then. I will see you later.

Nurse.
See you at the autopsy.

William Ash.
I will call you both when I am ready to sample the blood and to autopsy the organs.

[Exeunt Doctor and Nurse]

Enter Lindsay

Lindsay.
What happened to my husband?

William Ash.
It seems he was put into a trance by the ghost nymph and later died of explosive humiliation. We will be collecting samples soon to see how this happened because we want to know more. We would like to do an autopsy on the organs because of how your husband died. By the way, I am the only licensed medical examiner in this town.

Lindsay.
Okay, you can do the autopsy. I just want to know why my husband died.

William Ash.
It is a very unusual death. It could be the curse by Dorado. We don't really know who or what the ghost nymph is.

Lindsay.
So, you are saying the same thing can happen to me and my teenaged daughters.

William Ash.
Yes. All of you should be careful. The same thing

could happen to you and your teenaged daughters.
Don't hesitate to hide if you believe you could be
under attack.

Lindsay.
What should we do?

William Ash.
Just try and stay safe. It will be wise to remain calm.

Lindsay.
Is it possible to see the ghost nymph? I never saw this
so-called ghost nymph in my life.

William Ash.
It is possible that it is invisible to the naked eye. It
could appear for a few seconds and will then revert
back to its invisibility.

Lindsay.
Then how does it kill people?

William Ash.
I believe it could be due to an internal mechanism
within the body that sets off a ticking time bomb after
someone has seen the ghost nymph.

Lindsay.
Will someone turn to stone when it appears?

William Ash.
I believe it could put them into a trance and then an
internal mechanism will be set off in order to kill the
victim by explosive humiliation.

Lindsay.
Is that normal or proven?

William Ash.
Not yet, but that is my theory.

Lindsay.
Well, we will see you when we see you.

William Ash.
Just don't leave town because it could follow you.

Lindsay.
Will do.

[Exeunt All]

ACT IV

SCENE 1. Ashford, Connecticut. 1968.
House on a Plantation

Enter Narrator

Narrator.
There was a shock in the room. Lindsay and her two daughters did not know what to do. It is possible that Lindsay handled it better but the same can't be said about Cynthia and Abigail. It is such a surprise at what happened. But now something is about to happen.

Enter Cynthia

Cynthia.
What was that? It sounded like a scream.

Narrator.
It is already past midnight. Something is happening that no one knows about. Cynthia does not know what is going on.

Cynthia.
Hello, is anyone there? I have a gun and a flash light and am not afraid to use them.

Narrator.
And just then, there is something that has just happened. Cynthia sees an open door and enters the room.

Cynthia.
Hello. Oh My, Oh No! What has happened?
Ahhhhhhhh!

Narrator.
Cynthia calls the police because of what has happened
or what she believes has happened.

Enter Police Dispatcher

Cynthia.
Hello, police, I want to report a potential crime.

Police Dispatcher.
What would you like to report to the Ashford County
Police Department?

Cynthia.
I believe my mother and sister are unresponsive. I
believe something has attacked them. I don't know if
they are in a trance but their eyes are wide open. They
could be in a deep sleep but I don't hear them making
any noises. I don't even see them moving.

Police Dispatcher.
Where do you live?

Cynthia.
By the old plantation house.

Police Dispatcher.
Oh, that place again. We will send over someone you
might have been in contact with before.

[Exeunt Police Dispatcher]

Cynthia.
Whoever you are, we will find you soon.

Enter William Ash

William Ash.
Hello, is anyone in there? I am here again because of something mysterious that could have happened again.

Cynthia.
Oh, it's you. Come on in. I believe my mother and sister are unresponsive.

William Ash.
What was that?

Cynthia.
What was what?

William Ash.
You didn't hear that. Uh Oh.

Cynthia.
Why Uh Oh?

William Ash.
Stay close. I just heard a round of explosions somewhere close within this house.

Cynthia.
What do you think it could be?

William Ash.
It could be that pesky ghost nymph again.

Cynthia.
That thing again.

William Ash.
Well, it probably wants revenge or something.

Cynthia.
Well, I heard screams and then I went on check on my mother and sister, because it sounded like it was them getting nervous.

William Ash.
That information certainly helps. You said you heard screams? About how many times?

Cynthia.
About two or three

William Ash.
Were the screams loud or extremely loud?

Cynthia.
Extremely loud. They sounded high pitched. It sounded like someone was singing an opera. But the screams did settle to a lower pitch after a while.

William Ash.
It sounded like it was actually the ghost nymph who screamed.

Cynthia.
What makes you say that?

William Ash.
Well, the ghost nymph always has a high pitched

voice. It might seem it is from any one of your family members, only because the ghost nymph mimics the pitch and voice of everyone it wants to kill and or silence.

Cynthia.
Sounds intriguing

William Ash.
It is.

Cynthia.
Well, do you know where the explosions came from?

William Ash.
Just follow me.

Cynthia.
Do you think it could be in my mother's and sister's rooms?

William Ash.
Possibly, because that is where people are.

Cynthia.
So what are you going to do?

William Ash.
We must be very quiet. While the ghost nymph might have already been here, no one knows if she is still here. We could be next. The ghost nymph only makes herself known when she wants to kill or put people in a trance, which will eventually lead to that person dying due to shock.

Cynthia.
Are we nearing anything yet, since we are walking very slow?

William Ash.
We are almost there. We must walk slow to be very quiet. One loud movement might lead to the ghost nymph being alerted.

Cynthia.
Well, that makes sense.

William Ash.
Quickly, we must be quiet. We are here now. What room is this?

Cynthia.
That is my mother's room.

William Ash.
I am going to knock down the door now. Don't be frightened!

Cynthia.
What next, since you already knocked down the door?

William Ash.
We check on your mother. We need to know what has happened and we need to know now. I don't know how she died if she died, and I don't know if she was put into a trance. It is simply too soon to be known if we are not close enough. Her body might be under the bed sheets. Your mother might have exploded into pieces already

Cynthia.
What is that? I see blood near the windows and the ceiling.

William Ash.
I believe it is too late now.

Cynthia.
Well, I shouldn't have done that.

William Ash.
What? What did you find or see?

Cynthia.
I believe I found my mother's body. I believe she has already exploded into pieces.

William Ash.
Well, this is something else. Her body probably exploded into pieces within a matter of seconds or minutes after she saw the ghost nymph.

Cynthia.
What happens if the person who sees the ghost nymph is not frightened by the ghost nymph when she reveals herself?

William Ash.
I have never heard that. But it is possible that the ghost nymph might try something else or she could turn to stone or dust. But she could also disappear for the rest of eternity and be sent to hell or heaven. It is unsure if that ever happened but it will be interesting and or fun to watch.

Cynthia.
Well, that is something that I would like to see. It certainly seems like a possibility.

William Ash.
I see what happened.

Cynthia.
What did you find under the bed sheets?

William Ash.
I can see a pile of blood on the clean white bed sheets as well as the organs. The skin is everywhere in many different sizes and pieces. Blood is everywhere and I think it is something else. I believe it is your mother's body but somehow she reacted quickly. I need to collect this as evidence before I leave.

Cynthia.
What next?

William Ash.
We go to your sister's room. By the way, did you notice anything out of the ordinary in this room, and if you did, what was it?

Cynthia.
The windows were slightly opened and I could feel a chill on my body somewhere.

William Ash.
That is probably the sign of the ghost nymph or it could be the wind. We must be careful. It can turn into a nightmare. Now, let's go to your sister's room, so I can see her body.

Cynthia.
Ok. It is just down the hall and to the right and then down the left.

William Ash.
I see.

Cynthia.
I will take you there now.

William Ash.
So, this is your sister's room. It looks a bit larger.

Cynthia.
Well, this is just one of three master bedrooms. But each of the master bedrooms are different in size and shape.

William Ash.
What is that on the blades of the ceiling fan? Look up!

Cynthia.
I think that is my mother's head. How did that get here?

William Ash.
The ghost nymph could be telling us something. It is important that we not be scared.

Cynthia.
I am not scared. I just want to find my sister.

William Ash.
I see.

Cynthia.
There could be something else.

William Ash.
Wait, what's that leaking from underneath the bed sheets?

Cynthia.
It looks like blood.

William Ash.
I think the same thing happened to your sister. I am calling for back up. Your house is probably going to be condemned. If you have somewhere to go, you should leave now or in the next twenty-four hours or less.

Cynthia.
That will be fine. I already know where I am going to go. On the brighter side, today is my 18th birthday, but I don't know how I feel.

William Ash.
You should just relax. The backup will be here shortly. You should probably leave now while you can so you don't have to watch the investigation begin. You would not like what you see.

Cynthia.
I will leave now. All I will get is my suitcase, which is still packed mostly with my clothes, because I have yet to fully move in.

William Ash.
That will be fine.

Cynthia.
I grabbed my suitcase already and am taking a car to the airport. I will see you sometime in the future, won't I?

William Ash.
You will probably never see me again. But, I wish you well.

[Exeunt All]

SCENE 2. Connecticut. 1968.
Leaving Plantation For Airport

Enter Cynthia and Narrator

Cynthia.
I think I am going to the airport, but the closest one that is nearby. Good thing I have a fast car.

Narrator.
Cynthia drives off into the night and the police start to arrive to begin the investigation.

Cynthia.
It is apparent that something is happening at that house or plantation. It is possibly a curse, like either Dorado or one of the previous residents. There is still something that is strange and intriguing. I feel that I like this place but I don't know why I like it. There is just something to this place that I like and I don't want to know why. It will only be a matter of time that I will figure that out.

Narrator.
Cynthia just left a minute ago.

Cynthia.
What was that?

Narrator.
The ghost nymph reveals herself to Cynthia for a brief second.

Cynthia.
Was that the ghost nymph? I think it was. But why does nothing happen to me?

Narrator.
The ghost nymph laughs at Cynthia.

Cynthia.
Was that a manly laugh? Now that is very strange. I thought that ghost nymph was female?

Narrator.
The ghost nymph disappears and Cynthia finally arrives at the nearest airport, which is about two hours.

Cynthia.
I finally arrived at the airport, but I forgot my family was wealthy and had a private jet, so I will just fly it myself since no one is here and go to Fiji. But that ghost nymph situation was very strange. I believe that it was an evil and manly voice or laugh, whatever it was. Some things will just never change and I won't understand why.

Narrator.
Cynthia leaves the airport with the private jet, which is some long range plane that can reach up to 15,000 nautical miles without refueling but it is small and has the old primitive instruments. Yet, it has a very wide body but looks fat and short because of its length and wingspan.

Cynthia.
I think I will leave now. Good thing there is food on this plane.

Narrator.
Cynthia takes off and she arrives in Fiji the next day after seventeen hours of nonstop flying, of course with the autopilot on.

[Exeunt All]

SCENE 3. *Ashford*, Connecticut. 1968.
Anywhere Around Town

Enter Narrator

Narrator.
A week has passed since Cynthia left. But there is certainly a surprise.

Enter Abigail

Abigail.
Today is my eighteenth birthday. What am I going to do today?

Narrator.
Well, Abigail is back, but where did she ever go?

Abigail.
Since I am back in town I should probably see what's happening at that old house and plantation my parents bought. But I don't think I am going to spend that long in town.

Narrator.
It seems Abigail knows something about what is going on or she just doesn't care.

Abigail.
Well, what have we here. It appears something is happening to the house. It looks as though it is burning down or something.

Narrator.
Abigail is able to see the fire as she drives her car past the land. She does not think much of it but it is just not anything new.

Abigail.
Well, I guess I should go somewhere and disguise myself so people won't know who I am. But who knows me anyway in this dump of a town? Only about a few people. I don't even know where I am. After this I will take a long needed vacation.

Narrator.
Abigail wants to know what is happening to her parent's house but she doesn't want to get noticed, so she will just have to disguise herself.

Abigail.
Where will I go to get some fresh new clothes? I know, I will visit the next county over. It certainly looks like something is here that nobody wants the rest of people to know about.

Narrator.
Abigail drives two hours north.

[Exeunt All]

SCENE 4. *Salisbury,* Connecticut. 1968.
Anywhere Around Town

Enter Abigail and Narrator

Abigail.
It seems I am in Salisbury now. I wonder what is there. I need to find a mall or something but I don't know what is going on.

Narrator.
Abigail is able to find the town center and sees a bunch of food stands and grocery markets. There is no sign of any retail stores yet until she finally leaves the city limits.

Abigail.
I see there are no department/clothing stores in the city limits. Good thing I am out of the city limits and am in the county limits now. I think I see some type of boutique store. I guess I will go see what it is.

Narrator.
Abigail finally finds some store she likes.

Abigail.
I see a clothing store that looks like it sells boutique items. Let's see what they have before anything else goes wrong. There seems to be a nightmare occurring here for all the wrong reasons.

Narrator.
Abigail enters the store.

Enter Store Clerk

Store Clerk.
How may I help you?

Abigail.
I am looking for a wig, a short black-laced dress or something similar to it, a scarf, and some type of cosmetic product that would make my face feel flawless and young.

Store Clerk.
We have what you are looking for?

Narrator.
The Clerk hands Abigail the items.

Store Clerk.
Would you like to try on these items in the fitting room?

Abigail.
Yes

Store Clerk.
Follow me then

Abigail.
This store is bigger than I thought.

Store Clerk.
Oh Yeah! It might seem small, but all of the other stores that you see around this store are not real, because all of those stores are part of this store so that everything can be more efficient.

Abigail.
That seems interesting.

Store Clerk.
Ok. Here we are. First stall to the left.

Narrator.
The store clerk locks the door.

Store Clerk.
Push the button when you are done so I can open the door for you.

Abigail,
Okay

Narrator.
Abigail takes off her shirt and skirt and proceeds to put on a white-laced dress. And then she shortens her hair by braiding it and wraps the hair around the top of her head. Abigail then proceeds to place a wig cap given to her by the store clerk and then places the wig on her head. After that, Abigail wraps the scarf around her neck. It seems Abigail looks different but no one will know who she is.

Abigail.
Everything looks good on me. Now no one will ever recognize me.

Narrator.
Abigail pushes the button, which is hard to find at first, but she pushes it and it makes a chime only the clerk can hear.

Store Clerk.
Are you ready yet?

Abigail.
Yes.

Store Clerk.
Do you like what I selected or do you like something different?

Abigail.
I like everything. But I would like to also purchase a small purse or handbag and sun glasses.

Store Clerk.
Okay, that can be arranged. Do you want to wear it out or would you want to put it in a bag so you can wear it for the future?

Abigail.
I will just wear everything out. But I would like a bag for my clothes that I brought in here.

Store Clerk.
Okay. I am going to open the door now.

Abigail.
How do I look?

Store Clerk.
You look fabulous. I don't even recognize you.

Abigail.
I feel as though no one will notice me.

Store Clerk.
Probably. Follow me to the front of the store so I can ring you up.

Narrator.
Abigail and the store clerk arrive at the front where the cash register system is. It is an antique-looking system because everything is old fashion. Nothing is even computerized. The cash register seems like it is from the 1920s or 1930s because there were only a bunch of numbers and levers.

Store Clerk.
Okay. Your total will be $795.00. How will you like to pay?

Abigail.
Cash. I would like to pay cash.

Store Clerk.
Okay. I will press the cash button. Okay, it's set.

Narrator.
Abigail gives the clerk $800.00 and she counts it in front of her.

Store Clerk.
It seems you gave me $800.00. Would you like a receipt or something?

Abigail.
No, I'm fine. I don't need any receipt. You can keep the change as well. I don't really need it.

Store Clerk.
Okay. Hand me your clothes you wore in and I will give you a matching purse and a pair of sunglasses that you want as well.

Abigail.
Okay. Here you are.

Store Clerk.
Here are you pair of sun glasses and a small handbag you can wear.

Abigail.
Have a nice day.

Store Clerk.
See you soon.

Abigail.
Bye

[Exeunt Store Clerk]

Narrator.
Abigail exits the store and heads towards her car so that she can go back to Ashford to see what all the fuss is about at the house and plantation.

Abigail.

What a peculiar store? I guess everything is an illusion until you actually know what it is.

Narrator.

Abigail gets into her car

Abigail.

It seems I don't need anything here anymore. I am going back to Ashford now.

Narrator.

Abigail leaves in her car and arrives back at Ashford two hours later.

[Exeunt All]

SCENE 5. *Ashford,* Connecticut. 1968.
Anywhere Around Town

Enter Abigail

Abigail.

I see the house and plantation are still in a wreck

Enter Narrator.

Narrator.

Abigail passes her house that her parents just bought and sees that it is the same. She sees some new and old construction equipment. It seems just like it was yesterday, but it was still a week ago.

Abigail.
Where do I go now? It seems that there is something crazy about everything in this town.

Narrator.
Abigail decides to go to the police station because she might find answers there.

Abigail.
Off to the police station I go. I hope they know what is happening around here.

Narrator.
Abigail arrives at the police station.

Enter Police Officer

Police Officer.
How may I help you?

Abigail.
I want to know what is going on by or near the house and plantation.

Police Officer.
Oh, that old place. Well, there is not much to say. All we know is that there was a ghost nymph attack on it and everyone died inside who did not escape.

Abigail.
Sounds like something went on there.

Police Officer.
Something did go on there.

Abigail.
Seems logical. I passed by there while deciding where to go and I decided to come here because I believe the police should have a better understanding of the situation that is currently happening.

Police Officer.
We do know that.

Abigail.
There seems to be construction equipment there. What is going on there.

Police Officer.
It is set to be demolished because it is just too dangerous to live there.

Abigail.
Do you think it will be safe for anyone to ever go back there to live on?

Police Officer.
Probably not. We will probably just let the trees, bushes, and other plant life to overgrow there so that the animal life can thrive.

Abigail.
What about an officer named William Ash who is supposed to be a detective, sergeant, and lieutenant. I heard that he is in charge of this case.

Police Officer.
That person does not exist because he died over thirty-six years ago today.

Abigail.
Wait, are you sure?

Police Officer.
Yes. You probably saw a ghost or something because on this same exact day, he died in the line of fire, after being caught in a house fire that nearly killed me.

Abigail.
Well, that is a surprise. I probably won't be here anytime in the future, so see you when I see you, if I ever see you again.

Police Officer.
See you later, Abigail.

[Exeunt Police Officer]

Abigail.
Wait, how did he know my name. This is starting to get mysterious and strange. Oh Well, off to New Haven, where I will pick up my boyfriend, Hank, and then we go to the Caribbean.

Narrator.
Abigail arrives back at her old New Haven home and she picks up her boyfriend Hank.

[Exeunt All]

SCENE 6. *New Haven,* Connecticut. 1968.
At Home and Then Departing

Enter Abigail

Abigail.
I am finally back in New Haven.

Enter Hank

Hank.
Hello, Oh it's you! I missed you baby.

Abigail.
It was only a week or so.

Hank.
I know baby.

Abigail.
I took care of my family situation. I think I scared away Cynthia. As far as I know, Cynthia thinks I am dead.

Hank.
What now?

Abigail.
Well, we leave this crazy city or town and we go to the Caribbean.

Hank.
Oh, I like that. Yacht

Abigail.
Yacht.

Hank.
When do we leave?

Abigail.
Now or sometime today.

Hank.
That will be fine.

Abigail.
Cynthia is probably still here.

Hank.
What are we going to do about that girl?

Abigail.
I already planned something?

Hank.
What is it then?

Abigail.
I planned a traffic accident where someone will try
and cut her off while driving and then another car will
swerve at her car while she is trying to avoid the other
car.

Hank.
She wouldn't know what hit her.

Abigail.
Yes, and there's more.

Hank.
Which is…

Abigail.
Another car will strike the other car that hit Cynthia's car and then more cars will proceed to crash into each other.

Hank.
Mass casualties?

Abigail.
Yes. There will be mass casualties.

Hank.
Perfect. But what happens if Cynthia tries to escape?

Abigail.
Then someone will kill her with a gun thinking she is the person responsible for the accident.

Hank.
Good!

Abigail.
But hopefully, Cynthia will die when she is in her car, and that will be the end of that.

Hank.
That sounds like a good plan. When does it take effect?

Abigail.
It has already gone into effect.

Hank.
That is good.

Abigail.
Now, we will leave now so that we can go to the
Yacht, which is at the docks.

Enter Narrator.

Narrator.
Abigail and Hank leave for the docks and arrive in a
matter of minutes. There was never any ghost nymph,
because it was an illusion. The entire town of Ashford
was the underworld, but Cynthia and Abigail were the
only two people who were immune to the façade, but
it doesn't stop there, because everyone in Ashford is
actually a ghost and it doesn't appear on a map.
Cynthia actually never made it, because she got
caught in a traffic accident, which was planned by
Abigail, and Cynthia later died on the scene. Leaving
behind a mysterious mystery, Abigail is actually from
the underworld, because she disguised herself as a
child, in order to pretend to be an orphan. Abigail is
actually immortal and is from the dwellings of Hell,
but she is a sweet girl with a hot and gorgeous body,
along with a nice ass and that is what you guys will
think, well she is all of that, but she is also a witch,
and looks can be deceiving.

[Exeunt All]

ACT V

SCENE 1. *New Haven,* **Connecticut. 1968.**
Driving to the Docks

Enter Abigail and Hank

Abigail.
It is night now.

Hank.
Where are the docks?

Abigail.
About twenty minutes away from here but still in New
Haven.

Hank.
I think I see water now.

Abigail.
We are nearing the docks and I can see the yacht from
here.

Hank.
That small thing. I thought I remember the yacht
being much larger than that.

Abigail.
No, behind it. You are looking at the wrong boat.
Besides, we are still a mile away from the entrance of
the marina.

Hank.
Oh, now I see it.

Abigail.
We are here now.

[Exeunt All]

SCENE 2. *New Haven,* Connecticut. 1968.
The Docks. On Yacht

Enter Narrator

Narrator.
Abigail and Hank arrive at the docks in order to board the docks.

Enter Abigail and Hank

Abigail.
We leave in the morning.

Hank.
What do we do all night?

Abigail.
We drink and have fun.

Hank.
Like what type of fun?

Abigail.
The normal type of fun that involves rowdy antics and maybe antics that are sexual in nature.

Hank.
Oh, that normal stuff. Yeah, what type of drinks do we have on the yacht when we get there?

Abigail.
I believe Rum, Cognac, Gin, and Brandy. I think there is also Vodka.

Hank.
Seems about right.

Abigail.
I believe we are at the yacht now, which is right to the left of us.

Hank.
It's bigger than I remembered.

Narrator.
Abigail and Hank board the Yacht.

Abigail.
Let's start this party. We leave at sunrise tomorrow.

Narrator.
It is sunrise and Abigail and Hank left a second ago.

Hank.
See you later, or not.

Abigail.
Off to the Caribbean we go. I'm not sure what will happen to my belongings at the house but I don't really care.

Hank.
We are finally leaving this place, because I never liked this place anyway.

Narrator.
In a glimpse of their departure, they are never seen again, because they escape into the future of the night, which will end up in the delightful sea of humanity. Ashford never existed. It was a trap and it took people by surprise, and on the eve of the hanging of Dorado, everyone disappeared and anyone who lived in Ashford would later die, except if you were a witch. It never appeared on the map because it never existed, and in the Caribbean, a boat appears, but no one is on it, because Hank and Abigail are actually dead, and they have been dead for over seven hundred years. A laugh is heard and a laugh it is, because it is the laugh of an old witch and her black cat.

There is a cautionary tale to tell everyone, but no one is ever seen again. Nothing was like that used to be and the single thing of importance is that Ashford disappeared off the planet of this world after Abigail left. It would be surprising to you that everyone was a trick, implanted by Abigail, which it was, but Abigail wanted revenge, because of what happened to her over seven hundred years ago, which was, she was a human sacrifice because she was still a virgin, so thought the people of the town of Salem, Connecticut.

In the case of nothing ever happening, that is the precise link between haunted and not haunted. There was never any town of Ashford, Connecticut to begin with, because it disappeared off the planet of the world centuries ago, and El Dorado was a made up story invented by Abigail, because it provided an event to look for, a place of time to the ends of the world. There is something to think about but that will remain with the mind of the future. Everything will be determined by nothing but you, I am still waiting to begin training, yet again, and you are a fool, my friend.

[Exeunt All]

SCENE 3. *Kingdom of Bacornia, 1215*
Duchy of Bacornia

Enter Narrator

Narrator.
The real story has yet to begin, as this is just the beginning.

Once upon a time there were three villages and one duchy in the kingdom of Bacornia, that used to be controlled by the outrageous rulers of the other kingdom, but they were all killed by the villagers, because of their laws. The kingdom took over these three villages and promised them with respect, but you thought it ends here, well, there is more. In this current situation everything will turn out normal, but things are about to change, because the King is about to hold a festival for five straight days at the castle. Here, in the Duchy of Bacornia, Ella Lohrina once had the perfect family with no problems, but one day, her mother died, which forced her father to marry a semi-evil woman named Frances Siterina, who also had two twin daughters named Caterina and Helenia. Ella's new stepsisters were not that awful, but they made her do all of their chores. At some times in life, Ella did enjoy cleaning because she had nothing better to do, yet, her father died one week later.

Enter Ella Lohrina

Ella Lohrina.
(Singing)
Passing the forest, there always seems a tone of secrecy. Everything is changing, as the colors are clear. Soon it will be winter, as autumn is near. There is a change, that hinders the attitude, of a changing growth. The trees are bare. The forest is growing. In the midst of a wooded area, people seem frightened. As everything is changing, I can see that it is near. I have found my destination, as everything is right.

Narrator.
Ella is walking in the forest and can be seen singing but what does she see?

Ella Lohrina.
Who is there? There seems to be a chirping of some kind.

Enter Caterina and Helenia Siterina

Caterina Siterina.
Oh, this is good. Someone thinks she can sing. Well, that is the end of those fun and games. She won't be happy for too long.

Helenia Siterina.
Ella, Ella, where are you? I need my chores to be scheduled so I can avoid them.

Caterina Siterina.
Helenia, sister, have you seen what Ella is doing?

Helenia Siterina.
No, I have not. I am looking for her because I need her to finish my chores that I purposely forgot to do, because she is the one assigned chores.

Caterina Siterina.
Well, I can tell you where she is.

Helenia Siterina.
Well, where is she?

Caterina Siterina.
Oh, you never asked?

Helenia Siterina.
Yes I did; stop acting like an idiot.

Caterina Siterina.
Ok, fine. Ella is singing in the woods.

Helenia Siterina.
She is, is she? Well, that will have to end soon.

Enter Frances Siterina

Frances Siterina.
Where is that girl?

Caterina Siterina.
Oh mother, I found Ella singing in the woods and I already told Helenia. She seems too happy.

Frances Siterina.
Oh, that is certainly interesting. She can't be having too much fun. Well, her fun needs to end, and it needs to end now.

Caterina Siterina.
What are we going to do to her?

Helenia Siterira.
Yeah, what are we going to do to her?

Frances Siterina.
Well, we will make her life more miserable. And then when her father gets back here from the fair we will make sure she witnesses his death as we kill him in front of her. She will be begging us to stop.

Helenia Siterina.
When is her father due back?

Frances Siterina.
In two nights time.

Caterina Siterina.
Why kill? Isn't there a better way?

Ella Lohrina.
Chirping birds, flying across the sky, wind is near. Such happiness everywhere.

Narrator.
Ella arrives back home and she is greeted with disdain for some purpose.

Ella Lohrina.
I'm home. I'm happy to be home. Hello!

Frances Siterina.
Yes, you seem happy indeed, and that is bad, really bad, because no one can be happy as you. It just means people will walk all over you.

Ella Lohrina.
Happiness does not mean that. It means that people are content because you feel joy.

Frances Siterina.
Well, if you say it like that, you won't mind doing some chores of your stepsisters'.

Caterina Siterina.
Yeah, you will feel pain.

Helenia Siterina.
Tell it to her sister.

Caterina Siterina.
Yeah!

Helenia Siterina.
Yeah!

Frances Siterina.
Girls, don't say too much to her. She might get confused and will see then that she is not meant who she is meant to be. She needs to do everything slow so we can ruin her life. She will see that her ways are bad for the rest of society.

Ella Lohrina.
What am I to do?

Frances Siterina.
What you didn't do yesterday, today's chores, as well as chores for tomorrow.

Ella Lohrina.
But I already did yesterday's chores?

Frances Siterina.
Insubordination won't be tolerated.

Caterina Siterina.
Yeah, insubordination is bad!

Ella Lohrina.
Fine, I will do it.

Frances Siterina.
That's better.

[Exeunt All]

SCENE 4. *Kingdom of Bacornia, 1215*
Going to the Village of Anoniaponia

Enter Emily and Narrator

Emily.
Off I am to my grandmother's house in the woods with wine and cheese. I shouldn't but I might, drink the wine and eat the cheese, if I am thirsty and hungry.

Narrator.
Emily departed her house with the wine and cheese in
a medium-sized basket. So far she is staying on the
path but she hears a noise of some kind. Emily does
not know what it is but she has just entered the very
dangerous Enchanted Forest of Eleniaburnstad, a
place where she has never seen before.

Emily.
Hello! Is anyone there? I have wine and cheese if you
are interested.

Narrator.
Emily hears another noise. It sounds like an animal or
someone laughing.

Emily.
Hello again, is anyone there? I know you are here.
Show yourself now and I promise I won't hurt you, I
promise.

Enter Witch

Witch.
(Hiding Behind Trees)
Mwahahaha, mwhahaha, muahahaha, hehehehe,
bwuhuhuhaha.

Emily.
What was that? Please identify yourself.

Narrator.
And just like that, Emily's adrenaline increased
dramatically. Suddenly, someone appeared in front of
Emily.

Witch.
Hello, little girl! What are you doing here all alone here in the forest?

Emily.
I'm not afraid of you. I will just ignore you.

Witch.
You can't ignore me forever.

Emily.
Yes I can. I am going to my grandma's house and bringing her wine and cheese. And I'm not little, I'm almost 18.

Witch.
Well, you sure seem happy, but you shouldn't feel too happy.

Emily.
And why is that?

Witch.
Because, you might die soon.

Emily.
I'm not afraid of you.

Witch.
You should be

Emily.
I will not get stuck here.

Witch.
That is what you think.

Emily.
Why are you taunting me?

Witch.
I'm not taunting you.

Emily.
Yes you are.

Witch.
Well, what are you going to do about it?

Emily.
Nothing. I don't even know you.

Witch.
That's what I thought. You are scared.

Emily.
No I'm not.

Witch.
You could come with me and I will make you fresh-baked goods and candy. When you start smelling the food you won't be able to resist.

Emily.
I'm not interested. My mother never said to talk to strangers.

Witch.
Then, you are missing something very tasty and good.

Emily.
I don't really care about candy and baked goods that much, and besides I'm not interested in that right not, so you can stop it now.

Witch.
I will be waiting if you change your mind.

[Exeunt All]

SCENE 5. *Kingdom of Bacornia, 1215*
Village of Anoniaponia/Grandma's House

Enter Narrator and Emily

Narrator.
Emily finally arrived at her grandmother's house after nearly a one-hour delay due to getting off course and from talking to the witch.

Emily.
Grandma, I'm here to bring you some wine and cheese. Are you home?

Enter Simonia Bernfurt.

Simonia Bernfurt.
Hello, my dear grandchild. What have you brought to me?

Emily.
Why does your voice sound so different?

Simonia Bernfurt.
I have a cold.

Emily.
But then why is your voice a different pitch?

Simonia Bernfurt.
Because of my cold.

Emily.
But why?

Simonia Bernfurt.
Because I am going to cook you and then eat you,
along with your grandma.

Emily.
It's you.

Simonia Bernfurt.
Yes, I am that witch you met earlier today. I am
already prepping to cook your grandma.

Emily.
You won't get away with this.

Simonia Bernfurt.
Yes I will.

Emily.
Then where is my grandma? I don't see her.

Simonia Bernfurt.
She is supposed to be in the cauldron and I am
supposed to be lighting the fire shortly.

Emily.
Then why isn't she in there?

Simonia Bernfurt.
She is supposed to be tied up in the cauldron.

Emily.
Obviously, she isn't in there. I can see the cauldron from the kitchen and I can't see anyone in there. So, where is my grandma?

Simonia Bernfurt.
Maybe I ate her already.

Emily.
No you didn't She escaped.

Simonia Bernfurt.
Then prove it.

Emily.
I don't have to.

Simonia Bernfurt.
And why is that?

Emily.
Because she is right behind you.

Simonia Bernfurt.
You're lying, I don't see anyone.

Emily.
Then you're blind.

Simonia Bernfurt.
Tell me where she is, you little hooligan!

Emily.
No!

Simonia Bernfurt.
Well then, I guess you will die tonight, because I will cook you and eat you.

Emily.
You better think twice about that.

Simonia Bernfurt.
And why is that again?

Emily.
Because you are about to get knocked out and die.

Simonia Bernfurt.
How do you know this?

Emily.
Because my grandma is behind you with an ax and a pan.

Simonia Bernfurt.
You're lying.

Emily.
Well, you are going to find out shortly.

Narrator.
Suddenly, Simonia Bernfurt felt something behind her. She didn't know what it was.

Simonia Bernfurt.
What was that? Are you secretly a witch?

Emily.
Maybe I am, maybe I'm not.

Simonia Bernfurt.
You are trying to get on my nerves?

Emily.
Maybe

Simonia Bernfurt.
Well, stop it.

Emily.
Why should I.

Simonia Bernfurt.
Because I am your grandma.

Emily.
Then what is my name?

Simonia Bernfurt.
Emily

Emily.
And who told you that?

Simonia Bernfurt.
No one, dear.

Emily.
You're lying, my grandma told you my name, because
she knew I will be going to see her today.

Simonia Bernfurt.
You're very clever.

Emily.
And that is why you must die.

Simonia Bernfurt.
What was that? I will catch you and cook you so that I can eat you.

Emily.
No you won't.

Simonia Bernfurt.
And why is that, again?

Emily.
Because you are going to die tonight.

Simonia Bernfurt.
And how do you know that?

Emily.
Because my grandma has an ax and pan. She will knock you unconscious with the frying pan and will kill you with the ax.

Simonia Bernfurt.
Killing someone is against the law little girl.

Emily.
Not if it is self-defense. Besides, you won't even know when you are going to die.

Simonia Bernfurt.
You wish that will happen.

Emily.
Your wish is my command.

Simonia Bernfurt.
Are you some type of fairy now?

Emily.
Maybe, but I'm just human, so you figure it out for
yourself.

Simonia Bernfurt.
You are a strange little girl. Wait, I feel dizzy now.
Ouch, what was that? Uh, Oh! I think I am going to
faint now.

Narrator.
And with that, the witch known as Simonia Bernfurt
collapsed after Emily's grandma hit her with a pan,
and then proceeded to kill her with an ax.

[Exeunt Simonia Bernfurt]

Enter Grandma

Grandma.
Emily dear, I am happy you brought me some items?
What is it? Wine and cheese?

Emily.
Yes, grandma, it is wine and cheese. I hope you are
not in pain from that witch.

Grandma.

I'm fine dear. She was easy to distract. That was a very terrible witch who thought she could outsmart me, but I was already waiting for her because I have been hearing reports of missing children and people due to mysterious circumstances.

Emily.

Sounds interesting.

Grandma.

Yes it does. Are you interested in drinking this wine and eating this cheese with me before it goes all to waste.

Emily.

Yeah, okay. I'm starving. I was expecting a wolf not a witch.

Grandma.

I hear that the King is going to hold a five-night ball. You should go.

Emily.

Sounds fun. I might go.

Narrator.

With that, Emily and her grandma ate the wine and cheese and then Emily departed afterwards.

[Exeunt All]

ACT VI

SCENE 1. *Kingdom of Bacornia, 1215*
Village of Cynia/Going to Village of Elenia

Enter Narrator

Narrator.
Meanwhile, Jack, is getting ready to go into town to
the Village of Elenia to sell the family cow.

Enter Jack and Jack's Mother

Jack's Mother.
Go into town and sell our cow because we won't be
alive anymore if we can't eat.

Jack.
But, but! That cow is my best friend.

Jack's Mother.
Stop complaining. The cow is dying and we will have
no mon?

Jack.
No, mother.

Jack's Mother.
Make sure you get at least seven gold coins or
eighteen silver coins for the cow.

Jack.
Where do I go? There is more than one village or
town in this kingdom.

Jack's Mother.
Go to the Village of Elenia.

Jack.
Ok. I will see you later then.

[Exeunt Jack's Mother]

Narrator.
Jack leaves the Village of Cynia in order to go to the Village of Elenia to sell the cow.

Jack.
(Singing)
This place, is a place, that is a place. Where am I. Why did I go here. Where is my family. I am lost in the forest. This place is creepy. I want to find a way back out. There is nowhere to go. There is nowhere to hide. Anything can target you. There is a reason why people get lost in here. Do people survive., I have no clue. There is a way out, but it takes too long. I know I can escape this mysterious place, but why did I go here. It is time to exit this forest, once and for all, before anything else happens.

Narrator.
Jack arrives in town. He sees a man and asks him if he is willing to buy the cow.

Enter Mysterious Man

Jack.
Hello there, do you have any money to buy my cow? She is a good cow. My mother needs money.

Mysterious Man.
I think I have some money for your cow.

Jack.
How much are you willing to pay for my mother's cow?

Mysterious Man.
How much do you want?

Jack.
My mother either wants seven gold coins or eighteen silver coins.

Mysterious Man.
Okay. Let me check my pocket.

Jack.
No problem, I have nothing better to do.

Mysterious Man.
Okay. I have five gold coins and ten silver coins. I tell you what, I will give you these five gold coins and I will throw in something more that is worth more than these gold coins.

Jack.
What else will you offer?

Mysterious Man.
These mysterious beans that are worth seven gold coins each and I am giving you all seven of them, so together, I buy your cow for a total of 54 gold coins. This should make your mother proud.

Jack.
Thank you, kind sir. I can sell these beans to get money.

Mysterious Man.
That a boy. You go make your mother proud by redeeming the cash value of those means. By the way, I heard the King is ordering a ball for the next five nights.

Jack.
Isn't that for just the women who live in the kingdom?

Mysterious Man.
Maybe, but the King wants the prince to get married for some particular reason.

Jack.
Ok.

Mysterious Man.
Good luck.

[Exeunt Mysterious Man]

Narrator.
The mysterious man disappears with the cow as Jack puts the gold coins and beans into his pocket. Jack does not know it yet but he has been conned by a mysterious stranger. His mother is going to be angered when he tells her.

[Exeunt All]

SCENE 2. *Kingdom of Bacornia, 1215*
Village of Cynia

Enter Jack and Jack's Mother

Jack.
Mother, I'm home. I sold the cow for 5 gold coins and seven beans that are worth seven gold coins each.

Jack's Mother.
Are you mad? Why did you trade our cows for beans? I told you to sell it for more than five gold coins also. You let me down.

Jack.
But I can sell all of the beans for a total of 49 gold coins. They are magic.

Jack's Mother
Magic beans! Who told you that? The person who told you that?

Jack.
I said the beans were magic so that I will make more money when I sell them.

Jack's Mother
So, you are just going to swindle people out of their money. Face it, you are just as bad as the person who gave you those beans.

Jack.
But he also gave me 5 gold coins for the cow as well.

Jack's Mother.
But he did not give you 7 gold coins. He only gave you 5 gold coins and 7 beans.

Jack.
But the value of the beans and the gold coins are about 54 gold coins altogether.

Jack's Mother.
A bean does not cost 7 gold coins. It probably only costs 1/1000 of a silver coin. Face it boy, you got cheated.

Jack.
I wish I was never born.

Jack's Mother.
And I wish I had a daughter.

Jack.
Well, too bad, you're stuck with me. And you should be sad that I can't go to the King's ball.

Jack's Mother.
What ball?

Jack.
The person who gave me these beans says that there will be a ball for the next five nights.

Jack's Mother.
Well, too bad you're not invited, because these balls are only for women and not men. I could go in your place because I might find me a rich man there who will get me out of this mess.

Jack.
You are dreaming. No prince will marry you. Face it,
we are just peasants to them.

Jack's Mother
You're the one that is dreaming. You go to your room
now and think about what you did, and give me those
beans and five gold coins.

Jack.
Fine, I hope you're happy.

Enter Narrator

Narrator.
Jack gives his mother the gold coins and beans. She
throws the beans several yards away in the grass
pastures, as she deems them useless and worthless,
and then orders Jack to go to bed.

Jack's Mother.
Now, go to bed.

Jack.
With no supper?

Jack's Mother.
You don't deserve any supper because you did not
listen to be. You were conned.

Jack.
Fine! But I hope you're happy. I hope you die because
you upset me. I wish you were never my mother. You
never gave me a chance. I got you your gold and you
are still unhappy.

Narrator.
Jack goes to his room and shuts the door behind him.
But overnight, the beans grow into a beanstalk, and
Jack's mother awakens to something in her sight that
she doesn't recognize.

Jack's Mother.
Jack, wake up. Your beans grew into a beanstalk
overnight. I order you to chop it down with an axe
because that beanstalk is dangerous.

Jack.
Why me? And how do you know that it is dangerous?

Jack's Mother.
Because I climbed such a beanstalk before when I was
your age as well.

Jack.
But I am nearly 18.

Jack's Mother.
You are still 17. And I order you to chop it before the
giant and his wife try to eat us.

Jack.
Why are you telling me this?

Jack's Mother.
Because I stole from the giant and his wife when I was
16 and I told my mom that the beanstalk was very
dangerous because the giants were after me. If we
don't knock down the beanstalk now, we might die, as
they could remember me.

Jack.
And you are just telling me this now? Ok. I will get the axe. But I want to go into town tonight if you are going to the ball.

Jack's Mother.
That's if the King ever announces it to the people of the duchy and the three villages. It isn't official until the King's men announces it.

Narrator.
Jack gets an axe and chops down the beanstalk and it was a success. The giant and his wife fall to their deaths and never stood a chance.

[Exeunt All]

SCENE 3. *Kingdom of Bacornia, 1215*
Duchy of Bacornia.

Enter Narrator and Town Crier

Narrator.
The town crier of the Duchy of Bacornia arrives on horseback with royal soldiers.

Town Crier.
Here Ye, Here Ye. For five nights, starting tomorrow, all ladies, whether married or single, are invited to the royal palace to attend a royal ball in celebration of Prince Andre Eric Michael's engagement to lady Anna Rampione. All ladies are invited to attend, no matter your age. All married ladies may bring their husbands. Your sons and daughters are welcome as well.

Narrator.
Ella is watching the announcement and goes straight back home to tell her stepsisters and stepmother.

Enter Ella Lohrina and Frances Siterina

Ella Lohrina.
I just want to let you know that for the next five nights starting tomorrow, there will be a royal ball in order to celebrate the engagement between a lady and a prince, and that all ladies are invited.

Frances Siterina.
Good news girls, we are invited to a royal gala for the next five nights starting tomorrow. Maybe one of you two will get to marry the other prince.

Enter Caterina and Helenia Siterina

Caterina Siterina.
I will be the one to marry the other prince.

Helenia Siterina.
No, I will marry him.

Frances Siterina.
Girls, girls, we don't even know if the other prince is still in the market to get married.

Ella Lohrina.
I will be glad to go.

Caterina Siterina.
Awe, that's cute, she thinks the prince will marry her.

Frances Siterina.
You're not going unless you finish all of your stepsisters' chores, and if you finish those, I will make you do more chores. Besides, you will just be a big embarrassment to us.

Helenia Siterira.
Yeah, you will just be a big embarrassment.

Caterina Siterina.
What about El a's father? He is supposed to be back tonight.

Frances Siterina.
Oh, him! I decided to let him live for at least a week more.

Ella Lohrina.
What about my father?

Frances Siterina.
Sorry dear! But I'm afraid your father has died.

Ella Lohrina.
No he didn't. You and my stepsisters were going to kill him when he arrived back tonight. Wait until I contact the Royal Authorities.

Frances Lohrina.
And you won't tell anyone of this because you won't be going to the ball at all. Instead, you will be busy with too many chores. I was going to kill your father but I changed my mind when I heard about the five royal balls. But now, I think I am going just going to

keep him locked up when he arrives back.

Ella Lohrina.
You won't get away with this.

Frances Siterina.
Yes I will. Now go design our dresses.

Ella Lohrina.
But some way I will marry the prince if he is also interested in getting married.

Frances Siterina.
Dream all you want you poor child, but no one will believe a servant girl.

[Exeunt All]

SCENE 4. *Kingdom of Bacornia, 1215*
Duchy of Bacornia.

Enter Narrator

Narrator.
It was almost nightfall and a spy for Ella's father told him that the two stepsisters along with his wife were going to torture and kill him in front of Ella.

Enter John Lohrstadt and Charles Lohrina

Charles Lohrina.
Oh, Hello John. I haven't seen you for some time. Is everything okay or do you have something to tell me about back home. I can handle the news no matter how gruesome it might be.

John Lohrstadt.

Sir, I'm afraid your wife and the two stepsisters are
going to torture you and then kill you in front of Ella
when you arrive back home tonight. And then I also
found out that they changed their mind again but then
they changed their mind for a second time after Ella
stood up to your wife. Now, when you arrive back
tonight, you will supposedly be tied up. Your wife
was going to take you and her two daughters to the
royal balls for the next five nights, but she changed
her mind and is only going to take her two daughters.
She won't allow Ella to go because she does not like
her. You can still make it tonight.

Charles Lohrina.

Thank you John. You have been a great help. I guess I
will have to alert the authorities or something. Or I
could do nothing and will alert the authorities later via
my daughter after I get tied up.

John Lohrstadt.

Your pleasure, my liege. If I was you I would just play
along with being tied up. Just pretend to act up so it
will give Ella certain signals that you might already
know about the plan. Ella is planning to sneak out and
go to the five royal balls to see if the other prince
might be interested in marrying her or because she just
wants to get some fresh air since she is always not
allowed to do anything for herself.

Charles Lohrina.

Yes, indeed, John. I think I will go with that plan and
pretend to be frightened. Hopefully, Ella will pick up
certain signals and she will help me when the balls are
over.

John Lohrstadt.
Very good plan indeed sir. But won't you get tired of being tied up for six days? It will only take about an hour or so.

[Exeunt John Lohrstadt]

Narrator.
John and Charles parted ways. John went into town while Charles arrived back home about over an hour later.

Charles Lohrina.
Hello! Are there any lights on in there? Wait, who are you guys?

Narrator.
Two big strong men pick up and drag Charles to the attic and tie him up.

Charles Lohrina.
Where are you taking me?

Narrator.
The strong men refuse to answer.

Enter Frances Siterina.

Frances Siterina.
Hello dear, have you missed me?

Charles Lohrina.
Why did these two men pick me up and then dragged me here? Did you hire new guards?

Frances Siterina.
No dear. You were simply in the way. And I want to
make sure I am in charge. I was going to take you
with me tomorrow night and the four following nights
to the royal balls, but then I thought that you were not
worth it.

Charles Lohrina.
You won't get away with this.

Frances Siterina.
Strongmen, bring a wooden chair and tie his legs to it
so he can't escape.

Narrator.
The strongmen follow the orders and then they leave
after Frances Siterina leaves the attic. The two
strongmen are done with their job and get paid for
what they did.

[Exeunt Frances Siterina]

Enter Ella Lohrina

Ella Lohrina.
Father, you are back. What did she do to you?

Charles Lohrina.
My dear daughter. I am fine, but she had two
strongmen pick me up and dragged me after I arrived
back home right in front of our house. Anyway, I
received some information from a friend that my wife
would have me killed and or tortured. For now, I will
just play along so she doesn't notice a thing.

Ella Lohrina.
Yes, father, I overheard that conversation. She and her two daughters don't like us. She doesn't want me to go to the royal balls. All she wants is money and for one of her two daughters to marry the other prince who is not engaged.

Charles Lohrina.
I married a monster.

Ella Lohrina.
Don't worry about that. If I marry the prince then I can get us out of this mess.

Charles Lohrina.
Thank you dear.

[Exeunt All]

SCENE 5. *Kingdom of Bacornia, 1215*
Duchy of Bacornia.

Enter Narrator

Narrator.
It is the next day and Ella has to finish making the three dresses for her two stepsisters and her stepmother.

[Exeunt Narrator]

Enter Ella and Charles Lohrina

Ella Lohrina.
Good morning father! Today I have to finish hemming

the dresses. Except stepmother is not allowing me to attend.

Charles Lohrina.
Why? Is it because she thinks one of her two daughters will marry the other prince if he is available?

Ella Lohrina.
Yes. She is going to make me do chores. And if I finish them before it is time to leave, she is going to make me do more chores.

Charles Lohrina.
I will see if I can help you with the dresses, even though I am tied up right now.

Ella Lohrina.
Thanks Father, but I am used to doing this work plus more.

Charles Lohrina.
And all this time I thought you were being treated well by your stepmother and stepsister.

Ella Lohrina.
I don't blame you. I think she brainwashed you or you were always too busy being a spy. Isn't it obvious? Your friend is John Lohrstadt. I know him too well. He feeds our animals that stepmother wants to sell because she is greedy. If you ever died, she will fire all of the household staff. We are very well-off but she is very cheap. I will probably do all of the chores if you died, but even though the entire household staff is still employed, I will be the one doing mostly

everything.

Charles Lohrina.
Is it that obvious?

Ella Lohrina.
Yes

Charles Lohrina.
I will try to be in your life more.

Ella Lohrina.
Don't worry. I will be fine.

Charles Lohrina.
But why didn't you tell me this earlier?

Ella Lohrina.
She said no one would believe a house servant.

Charles Lohrina.
A house servant? But you are not a house servant.
You are from the upper class of society.

Ella Lohrina.
I know father. She just hates me. The stepsisters hate
me too.

Charles Lohrina.
Well, I will be here for you now.

Ella Lohrina.
When do you want to escape. I can help you out but
stepmother might be mad if you are not here. All of
them might suspect a thing. I might be punished due

to me not being here.

Charles Lohrina.
I will just stay here until the time is right. Besides, the prince might come here and ask for your hand in marriage. You do plan on going to the royal balls, do you?

Ella Lohrina.
Yes, father. I plan on going to all five of the royal balls. But I worry I might be found out by my stepsisters and stepmother. So, I will have to just disguise myself. But I will have to try and find a way to sneak out after I leave.

Charles Lohrina.
But what would you wear?

Ella Lohrina.
I guess I could always wish for something extravagant to wear. I doubt it will work but I will probably make a wish from a shooting star or on my mother's grave. I still don't know what I will do. I will probably fake cry when my stepsisters and stepmother tell me that I am not good enough to attend the royal balls. I will put on a dress before they leave and will then ask them how it looks. I believe they will say it will look horrible on me and that the dress resembles something that a peasant wears.

Charles Lohrina.
That is a good start. But she will probably make you do chores. Your stepmother has a thing with lentils, and I don't know why.

Ella Lohrina.
That is her favorite punishment chore for me.

Charles Lohrina.
And if you finish cleaning up those lentils or whatever it is, she might make a mess again and force you to clean it up again. Just be motivated and clean it up faster, but she might make you do it again. It looks like she does indeed hate you.

Ella Lohrina.
That is how I feel she might act. I think I am almost done with the third dress.

Charles Lohrina.
They look ok I guess.

Ella Lohrina.
What does ok mean?

Charles Lohrina.
They're fine but they look awful.

Ella Lohrina.
The stepsisters and stepmother asked me to go into town and get some dresses from a tailor. All I had to do was hem it a little, which is what I am doing now after I took into consideration the height and weight after they each tried on a dress.

Charles Lohrina.
Did they go with you?

Ella Lohrina.
No. I was just given money and told to pick up three

dresses. The dresses were already finished but were not tailored to specific measurement requirements, so I am hemming them.

Charles Lohrina.
Then, whoever designed the dresses have horrible taste.

Ella Lohrina.
I feel the same way but they liked the design. The design looks like it is for snobby people.

Charles Lohrina.
I agree.

Ella Lohrina.
I think they believe they are better than anyone else because my stepmother believes one of my stepsisters will have a chance to marry the other prince. They think that I am too poor.

Enter Narrator

Narrator.
Ella finishes hemming all of the dresses.

[Exeunt All]

SCENE 6. *Kingdom of Bacornia, 1215*
Duchy of Bacornia.

Enter Narrator and Ella Lohrina

Narrator.
As Ella finishes the dresses, she takes them downstairs

to her stepsisters and stepmother. It is still early but they are leaving in about two hours. So, it is very important for them to try them on to see if any alterations need to be made.

Ella Lohrina.
I'm done with the dresses.

Enter Caterina and Helenia Siterina

Caterina Siterina.
It's about time.

Helenia Siterina.
These dresses better fit.

Enter Frances Siterina.

Frances Siterina.
The dresses look fine but could be done better.

Helenia Siterina.
I better not look hideous.

Caterina Siterina.
Yeah!

Helenia Siterina.
I look gorgeous. The prince will have to marry me.

Caterina Siterina.
I look prettier than you. I will marry the prince.

Frances Siterina.
Girls, girls, you both have a chance to marry the

prince.

Ella Lohrina.
That's if he is available to be married.

Caterina Siterina.
What do you know about him?

Ella Lohrina.
I never said anything about knowing him.

Helenia Siterina.
Silly Ella. Always thinking that she can get the prince for herself.

Ella Lohrina.
I have nothing wrong. I think I have a good chance of well with the prince. I made a dress for myself.

Helenia Siterina.
This is great. It probably looks hideous.

Caterina Siterina.
People will stay away from you because you will look ugly in any dress.

Helenia Siterina.
No one would dance with a servant.

Enter Narrator.

Narrator.
Ella goes to her room and gets the dress and then puts it on.

Helenia Siterina.
What is that awful thing?

Caterina Siterina.
It looks hideous and terrible.

Frances Siterina.
That dress looks old and like garbage. I wouldn't be caught with you wearing that dress.

Ella Lohrina.
I can go too.

Frances Siterina.
Not with that dress. You would be an embarrassment to us all. Besides you need to take care of your father. You wouldn't want to be charged with murder.

Ella Lohrina.
But I have been very patient and extremely nice to all of you. My father doesn't even know what you are doing to me.

Helenia Siterina.
You weren't being nice, you were being very spiteful to us.

Ella Lohrina.
But I did your chores.

Frances Siterina.
And you won't be going, Ella.

Caterina Siterina.
Yeah, you won't be going, because you are not

welcome there. No one cares for a servant girl who
has zero friends.

Narrator.
Frances Siterina throws a dish of lentils for Ella to
clean up.

Frances Siterina.
If you can clean this up in two hours then you can go
to the royal balls.

[Exeunt Caterina and Helenia Siterina]

Narrator.
Ella finishes cleaning up the lentils in about half an
hour.

Ella Lohrina.
I'm done.

Narrator.
Frances Siterina is upset that Ella cleaned the mess up
so fast, so she throws another dish of lentils.

Frances Siterina.
You missed a spot.

Ella Lohrina.
You just threw that there.

Frances Siterina.
If you can finish it within one hour you can go with us
to the royal balls.

Narrator.
It takes about ten minutes for Ella to finish cleaning up the second mess of lentils.

Ella Lohrina.
I'm done.

Narrator.
The stepmother was angered and frustrated that Ella finished cleaning up the mess very quickly and so she and the stepsisters left for the first night of the royal ball.

Ella Lohrina.
Is anyone there?

Narrator.
Ella opens the front door and sees them leaving. Ella is stunned.

[Exeunt All]

ACT VII

SCENE 1. *Kingdom of Bacornia, 1215*
Duchy of Bacornia

Enter Narrator and Ella Lohrina

Narrator.
It is one minute after dark and Ella quickly gets some bread and milk for her father to eat and drink.

Ella Lohrina.
Here you are father. They left without me and they did not want to be seen with me.

Enter Charles Lohrina

Charles Lohrina.
Thank you dear. It is a beautiful dress, but I guess they called it hideous.

Ella Lohrina.
Yes, they did call it that. I still plan on going but I will just pray on my mother's grave.

Charles Lohrina.
That's the spirit. Maybe your wish will come true. I will be fine.

Ella Lohrina.
Thank you father. I too will be fine. I just want to get as far away from here as possible if I can.

Charles Lohrina.
That's a girl.

Ella Lohrina.
Thank you again father.

[Exeunt Charles Lohrina]

Narrator.
Ella goes to her mother's grave and wishes that she can go to the royal balls. She waits a minute and starts to cry, but her wish is granted. A gold and silver dress drops from the sky as well as a pair of silk shoes. But it is from white birds.

Ella Lohrina.
Oh, thank you, whoever you are. Oh, it's you! Thank you my white bird friends.

Narrator.
Ella puts on the dress and shoes and then leaves to attend the first night of the royal ball but she knows she has to leave the ball before her stepmother and stepsisters leave.

[Exeunt All]

SCENE 2. *Kingdom of Bacornia, 1215*
Duchy of Bacornia/Royal Castle

Enter Narrator

Narrator.
Ella arrives at the first night of the royal balls and she walks up the stairs and is greeted by the royal soldiers

and the rest of the staff. Ella sees many ladies and princesses but cannot see her stepmother or stepsisters because she is not close enough.

Enter Ella Lohrina

Ella Lohrina.
Wow! I wonder if I can find the prince.

Enter Herald

Herald.
Announcing, the Prince, Andre Eric Michael and his future bride, lady Anna Rampione.

[Exeunt Herald]

Narrator.
Anna and the Prince begin to dance. Meanwhile, Prince Henry David Michael can see Ella from atop of the royal staircase standing in the balcony. Ella can see him and the prince can't believe that he saw someone that beautiful.

Enter Henry David Michael

Henry David Michael.
Wow, look at that! Isn't she beautiful?

Narrator.
Ella descends the stairs and is greeted by the prince. She is fascinated by his appearance and he is also fascinated by her appearance. It looks as though this even was made for her.

Ella Lohrina.
Wow! You look amazing!

Henry David Michael.
I have never seen a more beautiful lady.

Ella Lohrina.
Thank you.

Henry David Michael.
Shall we begin dancing?

Ella Lohrina.
Oh, Yeah!

Narrator.
Ella and the prince dance the first night together.

[Exeunt Ella Lohrina and Henry David Michael]

Enter Anna Rampione & Andre Eric Michael

Anna Rampione.
Wow! She looks amazing. Who is she?

Andre Eric Michael.
A mysterious maiden who is beautiful.

Anna Rampione.
She is something. She looks amazing.

Andre Eric Michael.
It seems my brother also has good taste in women.

Anna Rampione.
You can say that again.

[Exeunt Anna Rampione & Andre Eric Michael]

Enter Herald.

Herald.
Announcing, lady Emily of Elenia, accompanied by Jack of Cynia.

[Exeunt Herald]

Enter Emily and Jack

Emily.
Who is that girl?

Jack.
It looks like some type of mysterious princess.

Emily.
I like her dress. Don't even think about going over there?

Jack.
Why?

Emily.
Because, she looks too good for you, and we don't even know who she is.

Jack.
I wasn't think about going over there anyways, and you already knew that.

Emily.
You are much smarter than you look.

Jack.
So, when are we going to dance?

Emily.
When your mother stops flirting with all of the men near that mysterious girl.

Jack.
Fair enough.

Enter Ella Lohrina

Ella Lohrina.
What time is it?

Narrator.
Emily is nearby and can hear Ella.

Emily.
It is almost midnight. But who are you?

Ella Lohrina.
That is not important right now. I just need to leave before I get noticed by people who I know.

Emily.
Ok then.

Ella Lohrina.
Bye then.

Jack.
Why were you talking to her?

Emily.
I don't know. I think she knows someone here and is trying to run away and go back home before she gets noticed.

Jack.
Sounds like someone is afraid of getting caught.

Emily.
Or she isn't who she says she is.

[Exeunt Emily and Jack]

Narrator.
Ella quickly walks down the grand staircase after she exits the royal palace and goes back to her home where she will take care of her father.

Ella Lohrina.
(Singing)
It is almost midnight. It is almost midnight. I need to get home soon before someone finds me. I need to get home to see my father. It is almost midnight. I need to see my father. I need to get home so no one even knows that I was ever gone. I am home now but I am here. I am home before midnight.

[Exeunt All]

SCENE 3. *Kingdom of Bacornia, 1215*
Duchy of Bacornia

Enter Charles and Ella Lohrina

Charles Lohrina.
How was the first night of the royal ball?

Ella Lohrina.
It was fine. I met the prince. I danced with him all night. It was a very nice night.

Charles Lohrina.
Sounds like you had a great time. Are you going back tomorrow?

Ella Lohrina.
I might.

Charles Lohrina.
That's my girl.

Ella Lohrina.
Wait, I think I hear my stepsisters and stepmother arriving home.

Charles Lohrina.
Go see what they are up to.

Ella Lohrina.
I will. See you later.

Charles Lohrina.
Good luck!

[Exeunt Charles Lohrina]

Enter Frances Siterina

Frances Siterina.
Oh, there you are my dear. Sorry you had to miss the
first night of the ball.

Ella Lohrina.
It wasn't that special, was it?

Enter Caterina and Helenia Siterina

Caterina Siterina.
Why are you smiling, Ella?

Helenia Siterina.
Yeah, do you know something, Ella?

Frances Siterina.
Girls, girls, she is probably acting mad because she is
cleaning too much.

Ella Lohrina.
What did I miss anyway?

Caterina Siterina.
You probably wouldn't care.

Helenia Siterina.
There was this girl or princess at the ball dancing with
the prince all night long, and her dress was just too
beautiful to ignore.

Caterina Siterina.
No one knew who she was. I wish I got closer so I could recognize her.

Frances Siterina.
She must be some type of princess with very good taste. I don't know who she was but I want to know. I want that dress for one of my daughters.

Ella Lohrina.
Sounds like all of you had a great time.

Caterina Siterina.
We did, but we would have had a greater time, if it wasn't for that mysterious princess or girl who showed up.

Helenia Siterina.
Yeah, she ruined the night.

Ella Lohrina.
Sounds like someone was jealous.

Caterina Siterina.
Well, she did ruin the night.

Frances Siterina.
And then she had the nerve to leave the prince and runoff somewhere.

Helenia Siterina.
I wouldn't have treated the prince that way.

Caterina Siterina.
Yeah!

Frances Siterina.
Besides, we don't know who she is

Caterina Siterina.
If she shows up at the royal ball again and does the same thing, I am going to try and see who she really is.

Narrator.
The next night arrives and Ella departs once again for the royal ball.

[Exeunt All]

SCENE 4. *Kingdom of Bacornia, 1215*
Duchy of Bacornia/Royal Castle

Enter Narrator and Frances Siterina

Narrator.
Ella arrives at the royal ball for the second night in a row. She sees her prince and starts dancing, while Ella's stepmother and stepsisters spot her again with the prince as well.

Frances Siterina.
Her again? What does the prince see in such a girl. It seems he is blinded by her beauty and cares about no one else.

Enter Caterina and Helenia Siterina

Caterina Siterina.
Her again.

Helenia Siterina.
She is just going to ruin the fun again.

Frances Siterina.
Relax, girls, she probably has nothing better to do.

Helenia Siterina.
She is probably a gold digger then.

Caterina Siterina.
So, she is trying to do the same thing as us.

Frances Siterina.
It appears so.

Caterina Siterina.
Well, I won't let her get away this time. I am going to try and get her before she runs away again.

Helenia Siterina.
What happens if she forgets to run away?

Caterina Siterina.
Well, we will have to make her run away then.

Frances Siterina.
Someone needs to teach her a lesson.

[Exeunt Caterina and Frances Siterina]

Helenia Siterina.
Hello, who are you?

Narrator.
Helenia asks Emily a question, mistaking her for Ella,

but Emily responds and tells her that she is probably mistaken.

Enter Emily

Emily.
I'm Emily. Why do you ask?

Helenia Siterina.
Never mind, I thought you were someone else.

Emily.
Where you looking for the mysterious princess or girl who just left again?

Helenia Siterina.
Yes. She left again?

Emily.
About one minute ago. She must be hiding from someone.

[Exeunt Helenia Siterina]

Enter Jack

Jack.
Who was that?

Emily.
Just someone who was looking for that mysterious princess or girl. She probably wants to find out more who that girl is. Whoever that girl is who danced with the prince again, well the other girl must be jealous or something.

Jack.
She must be because she wanted to probably ask her
something before she mysteriously disappears again
for some reason.

Emily.
Right you are.

[Exeunt Emily and Jack]

Enter Frances and Caterina Siterina

Caterina Siterina.
Well, where is she?

Frances Siterina.
Is she even still here?

Enter Helenia Siterina.

Helenia Siterina.
She left a few short minutes ago.

Frances Siterina.
Again! She must be hiding from someone.

Caterina Siterina.
Now my plans to dance with the prince are ruined
again.

Helenia Siterina.
Your plans? You must be dreaming. I will marry the
prince and you will not be invited to the wedding,
since you also want to ruin my plans.

Frances Siterina.
Girls, stop fighting. We will just have to wait for the
final royal ball and see what happens when she leaves.
The prince might go after her.

Caterina Siterina.
Fine, but I won't be happy about it.

Helenia Siterina.
I will be waiting for too long. Fine, but I won't be
happy either.

[Exeunt All]

SCENE 5. *Kingdom of Bacornia, 1215*
Duchy of Bacornia

Enter Narrator

Narrator.
The stepsisters and stepmother arrive back home just
minutes after Ella arrives back.

Enter Caterina Siterina and Helenia Siterina

Caterina Siterina.
That mysterious girl had to ruin my night again.
Where did she get that gold and silver dress. I mean, it
is more expensive than my dress.

Helenia Siterina.
More expensive than your dress? What about mine?
We don't even know where she got it. She could have
stolen it.

Caterina Siterina.
Well, why didn't you ask her? Oh, I know. Because she ran away again.

Enter Frances Siterina.

Frances Siterina.
That girl is going to ruin my plans.

Enter Ella Lohrina

Ella Lohrina.
Hello! How was the royal ball again?

Caterina Siterina.
It was ruined again. That girl showed up again and then left the prince, again. I didn't get to even dance with the prince because she danced with him for the entire night again.

Frances Siterina.
Someone should teach that girl a lesson.

Helenia Siterina.
Yeah! Someone should teach her a lesson, a lesson that says no one but us can dance with the prince. It is about time we find out who she is.

Frances Siterina.
But how?

Caterina Siterina.
I know. We can kidnap her before she escapes again. We must be very sneaky.

Ella Lohrina.
Maybe she needed to go home and rest.

Frances Siterina.
Well, she is certainly rude about it.

Caterina Siterina.
Not to mention she is wearing that same gold and silver dress.

Helenia Siterina.
Yeah! Where did she get that dress? I bet it would look gorgeous on me.

Helenia Siterina.
No, it will look better on me.

Ella Lohrina.
How about me?

Frances Siterina.
Ha, Ha, Ha, Ha, Ha, Ha!

Caterina Siterina.
You, wearing that dress? It would look hideous on you.

Helenia Siterina.
That dress wouldn't be right for you. It would ruin your appearance and make you look uglier. And you would be even more of a nuisance.

Frances Siterina.
You would embarrass our name and family and we would be the laughing-stock of the kingdom.

Ella Lohrina.
Well, anything is possible.

Frances Siterina.
Yes, but not for certain people.

Narrator.
The stepsisters and stepmother go to their rooms to get
undressed and then fall fast asleep.

[Exeunt All]

SCENE 6. *Kingdom of Bacornia, 1215*
Duchy of Bacornia

Enter Narrator and Ella Lohrina

Narrator.
It is the fifth and last final royal ball, and Ella just left
the royal castle again for a final time. But this time the
prince ordered pitch to be poured on the lower portion
of the staircase.

Ella Lohrina.
The prince poured pitch on the staircase. Now I am
stuck or I can leave the shoe behind. I don't know
what I am going to do. Wait, I should go now before
it's too late. I will just leave one shoe to find so he
will remember me.

Narrator.
Ella leaves one of her shoes behind and runs off back
home.

Ella Lohrina.
I am back home now and I plan to stay here awhile. I just want to wait to see if anything happens.

Narrator.
Ella just enters the house in time and removes her dress and places it in a hidden location and then puts on her old house outfit.

Enter Henry David Michael

Henry David Michael.
I will find her. She left her shoe behind. I will find her so I can marry her immediately. Should we wait or go in the morning?

Enter Herald.

Herald.
We should go now before something happens to her. It is nearly the morning, as it is only a few minutes to sunset.

Henry David Michael.
This is the longest time she danced with me. We shall depart immediately.

Narrator.
The prince and his knights go into town to find the maiden who fits the golden silk slipper.

Henry David Michael.
To all town folks, I am looking for a fair maiden who will fit into this golden silk slipper. I will marry her the next day after I find her.

Narrator.
The stepsisters and stepmother hears the arrival of the prince and they wait. The prince visits the house of Ella.

Enter Caterina Siterina

Caterina Siterina.
Why won't it fit?

Enter Frances Siterina

Frances Siterina.
Oh, Well, I guess some of your toes need to be chopped off.

Caterina Siterina.
Ahhhhhhhhhhhhhhhhhhhhh. It fits.

Herald.
Wait, is that blood I see?

Henry David Michael.
It is blood. Next maiden please

Enter Helenia Siterina

Helenia Siterina.
I'm trying to make it fit but it is just too tight.

Frances Siterina.
Oh, Well. Time to cut off some of your heel, my dear daughter Helenia.

Helenia Siterira.
Ahhhhhhhhhhhhhhhhhhhhh. It fits me.

Herald.
Wait, the birds have alerted me to blood again.

Henry David Michael.
Madam, two of your daughters have cut off part of
their feet to force the slipper onto their feet. We
thought they fit but it turned out birds from above got
my men's attention and alerted them to blood. So, I
ask you, do you have some other maiden living with
you in your house?

Frances Siterira.
Well, we keep a kitchen maid.

Henry David Michael.
I demand to see her.

Frances Siterira.
Ella, the prince needs you to try on a shoe.

Ella Lohrina.
The prince. I will be there. Ok, I am here.

Henry David Michael.
I ask you to try on this golden silk slipper.

Narrator.
The prince places Ella foot in the golden silk slipper
and it fits.

Ella Lohrina.
It fits.

Henry David Michael.
It fits. I shall marry you immediately. Right now, I need to take you back to the castle.

Narrator.
Suddenly, the stepsisters are attacked by the birds from above, and then a minute later, both of them suffer from heart attack and die immediately. And when the prince leaves with his men and Ella, the stepmother faints and dies from cardiac arrest, due to shock and surprise. But, before Ella tried on the slipper and went outside she untied her father and told him the prince will marry her.

It is the next day and Ella gets married to the prince, and it is a happily ever after, or so you thought, but there is something else in mind.

[Exeunt All]

SCENE 7. *Kingdom of Bacornia, 1219*
Royal Castle

Enter Narrator and Ella Lohrina

Narrator.
Four years have passed since the two royal weddings, and it is not as you have expected. There is something about the craziness of everything. It is about that time when everything goes wrong because you thought everything was going right. There is no one to stop it from happening because everything will eventually be implemented as it was originally designed for. It is for that reason why people must die in this story you thought was going to end happy.

Ella Lohrina.
(Singing)
Oh my, Oh dear. I got everything I ever wanted. I am married to the prince of my dreams. I have all I ever wanted. My stepsisters are dead. My stepmother is dead. My father is arrive. I have a happy life now but I don't feel happy. I want to explore the world. I want to have more adventure. I want to be more free. I got everything I ever wanted but I just want something more.

Narrator.
Ella decided to leave a letter to her beloved prince, saying she is leaving him to experience the world. It is nothing short of dangerous.

Enter Henry David Michael

Henry David Michael.
(Reading Letter from Ella)

"Dearest love,"
"I have decided to leave the castle because I feel empty inside. I feel like something is missing. It's not you, it's me. I just want to have more adventures. I want to experience the world. I want to learn more. I just need some time alone but I will be back when the time is right."

"Yours Truly, '

"Your Ella"

Narrator.
The prince read the letter and felt as though he let her

down. He tells his brother that he is leaving to find Ella.

Henry David Michael.
Brother, my Ella has run away to experience more adventure. She says she feels empty insider and it is not me but her.

Enter Andre Eric Michael

Andre Eric Michael.
You want me to tag alone with me? Should I bring my Anna or at least notify her?

Henry David Michael.
That is up to you, my brother.

Andre Eric Michael.
Ok, I will see if she wants to go.

Enter Anna Rampione

Anna Rampione.
What's wrong, my dear?

Andre Eric Michael.
Anna has decided to run off somewhere in order to experience the world. So, if you want, you can come with me and my brother to find her.

Anna Rampione.
Ok. I will get dressed now. How long until we leave and do we know where she is?

Andre Eric Michael.
We leave in three minutes.

Narrator.
Anna is ready and she and the two princes depart on horses.

[Exeunt All]

SCENE 8. *Kingdom of Bacornia, 1219*
Looking for Ella Lohrina

Enter Henry David Michael

Henry David Michael.
Oh, Ella, my dear, where are you?

Enter Andre Eric Michael

Andre Eric Michael.
Ella, can you hear us?

Enter Narrator

Narrator.
The princes and the princess Anna Rampione are looking for the princess Ella Lohrina but they are nearing the Enchanted Forest of Eleniaburnstadt. It is such a dangerous path they are on now.

Henry David Michael.
Where are we?

Andre Eric Michael.
I don't know where this place is. It looks like a

strange forest that is creepy and spooky. It looks familiar but I am just not sure.

Enter Anna Rampione

Anna Rampione.
I know where we are.

Henry David Michael.
You do! Well, where are we?

Anna Rampione.
This is the Enchanted Forest of Eleniaburnstadt. I went here sometimes before I met you. Both of you probably don't remember it because it wasn't that dark when you traveled here. Even though it is almost morning, the entire forest still stays dark until midday. And when the sun goes down, the forest immediately turns dark.

Andre Eric Michael.
But why the strange name?

Anna Rampione.
No one knows

Henry David Michael.
Well, if it is enchanted, it must be dangerous or at least contain magical creatures.

Anna Rampione.
I have only seen the regular forest animals. Maybe it is just a name to scare people. It isn't that scary, but some say once you enter you can never escape. But I don't believe that.

Henry David Michael.
Ok then! Well, let's keep moving.

Narrator.
All three move on and then see two people sitting in the middle forest and then stop again.

Anna Rampione.
You there, don't I remember both of you attending the royal balls four years ago?

Enter Emily and Jack

Emily.
Yes. Your hair is still long and beautiful.

Jack.
I do remember you as well.

Anna Rampione.
Great! Have you seen a girl that might of passed by anytime recently?

Emily.
You just missed her.

Henry David Michael.
How long ago?

Jack.
About three minutes ago.

Emily.
You won't find her if you continue on horse. You must walk to find her.

Andre Eric Michael.
Can you lead us to her?

Jack.
Yes!

Emily.
Just follow us.

Narrator.
The princes and princess get off of their horses and
follow Emily and Jack.

Henry David Michael.
Why are you two out here anyway?

Emily.
I'm just tired and wanted to experience something
new.

Andre Eric Michael.
How about you?

Jack.
I just feel tired of everything and want to get out
more.

Henry David Michael.
Fair enough!

Anna Rampione.
Don't you feel content?

Emily.
Well, I just feel something is missing.

Jack.
The same for me.

Emily.
Stop, now, we're here!

Henry David Michael.
Where is here?

Jack.
You will see soon. We will go with you.

Narrator.
A portal is opened and all enter it, not knowing what it
will lead to.

[Exeunt All]

SCENE 9. El Dorado, North America. 1354
Enchanted Forest.

Enter Narrator

Narrator.
All five are transported to the future, of what is known
as El Dorado. The year is now 1354, but they are still
in the same place, but it is just named differently due
to tribal naming issue.

Enter Emily

Emily.
Welcome to the future. You might like it here, but
Ella is just ahead, if you can see her. But first, you
must know we need to kill an evil witch doctor by the

name of Dorado so that we can live here for the rest of
our lives. We are still in the same place, but it is just
known differently.

Enter Henry David Michael

Henry David Michael.
The future. Okay!

Enter Andre Eric Michael

Andre Eric Michael.
Where is this witch doctor?

Enter Jack

Jack.
He is near.

Enter Anna Rampione

Anna Rampione.
I think I see someone nearby.

Emily.
Can you see who it is?

Anna Rampione.
I think it is Ella tied up to a tree.

Henry David Michael.
That is Ella.

Andre Eric Michael.
What should we do?

Emily.
We shouldn't make a noise or Dorado will do the same to us.

Henry David Michael.
Is Dorado the witch doctor you speak of?

Jack.
Yes!

Anna Rampione.
Where did he go?

Emily.
Uh oh! That means he has spotted us.

Jack.
Look out behind you.

Narrator.
Dorado ties up everyone up to a tree but Emily ran away before he could get her.

Ella Lohrina.
Oh, hey! You got caught as well? Wait, where's Emily?

Jack.
She ran off somewhere.

Enter Dorado

Dorado.
What was that? To the person who hit me, show yourself now, so I can kill you first.

Emily.
You can't find me.

Dorado.
Whoever you are, stop it now. As for the rest of you, I am going to feed you sweets and baked goods until you get fat, and then I am going to eat you.

Narrator.
But, suddenly, Dorado collapsed and turned to ash once more, after Emily hit him with a frying pan and an ax she found in a small cabin with a fireplace and a kitchen. And then she burned the witch doctor, which is why he turned to ash.

[Exeunt Dorado]

Emily.
Hold on guys! I will untie you from the trees now.

Henry David Michael.
Thank you, Emily!

Andre Eric Michael.
Thank you, Emily!

Anna Rampione.
Thank you, Emily!

Ella Lohrina.
Thank you, Emily!

Jack.
Thank you, Emily!

Emily.
You're welcome, guys!

Anna Rampione.
Well, what do we do now?

Jack.
We could all stay here.

Ella Lohrina.
I would like that very much.

Henry David Michael.
But what about our responsibilities in the kingdom of
Bacornia?

Emily.
It is still the same place, but we are only in the future,
of about a little over one-hundred years.

Andre Eric Michael.
Fair enough!

Henry David Michael.
I could live with that.

Anna Rampione.
I'm fine with that.

Ella Lohrina.
I can experience more adventure here.

Jack.
Ok, I can get used to this.

Emily.
Good! It's settled! We can all live here now and start a new kingdom.

Narrator.
With that, they all lived happily ever after.

Henry David Michael.
Hey, who said that?

Anna Rampione.
I think he is talking about us.

Enter Other Narrator

Other Narrator.
I didn't say anything.

Emily.
You are not the same person. There is more than one person.

Narrator.
Suddenly, the other narrator tried to hide.

Anna Rampione.
Just shut up, whoever you are.

Narrator.
Ok, fine! You can have my job if you want to. I give up on you guys.

Emily.
Thank you, Mr. Narrator.

Ella Lohrina.
With the curse lifted, the future of Ashford will prosper for many years to come. All of us have decided to stay here in order to build a new and more prosperous kingdom. Henry and I became the King and Queen, with Andre and Anna as second in line, and Emily and Jack as third in line.

Jack.
Wait, a curse, lifted?

Henry David Michael.
What curse? Oh well!

Andre Eric Michael.
We were all doomed?

Anna Rampione.
Mr. Narrator, take it away!

Narrator.
In the end, everybody lived happily ever after, and it was the best situation a romance could bloom.

The End!

[EXEUNT ALL: FINAL TIME]